Praise for

The Dirt Diary

"Holy fried onion rings! Fun from beginning to end."
—Wendy Mass, *New York Times* bestselling author of
11 Birthdays and *The Candymakers*

"I LOVED it…sweet, sensitive, and delicious!"
—Erin Dionne, author of *Models Don't Eat Chocolate Cookies*

"Confidently addressing a number of common tween troubles…[a] humorous problem novel."
—*Publishers Weekly*

Praise for
The Prank List

"*The Prank List* hooks readers with snappy dialogue from the beginning... Rachel is a likable character for middle-school readers, who will relate to her problems."

—VOYA

"Staniszewski keeps the focus on comedy...but she lets her story become a bit more serious with the pranks Rachel plays. Gentle...fun laced with equally gentle wisdom."

—Kirkus Reviews

"Tween readers who find Rachel endearing will find a fast-paced comedy of errors."

—School Library Journal

Praise for
My Very UnFairy Tale Life

"Anna Staniszewski creates a magical world that's totally relatable. You'll find yourself wishing you were alongside Jenny fighting against unicorns (who aren't as peaceful as you think) and traveling to fantastical realms."

—GirlsLife.com

"A light comic romp… An eye for imaginative detail mixes with these likable characters and a theme of empathy… Charming."

—Kirkus Reviews

"Staniszewski's debut is a speedy and amusing ride that displays a confident, on-the-mark brand of humor, mostly through Jenny's wisecracking narration…will keep readers entertained."

—Publishers Weekly

Also by Anna Staniszewski

The My Very UnFairy Tale Life series

My Very UnFairy Tale Life

My Epic Fairy Tale Fail

My Sort of Fairy Tale Ending

The Dirt Diary series

The Dirt Diary

The Prank List

The Gossip File

I'm With Cupid

SWITCHED AT
FIRST
KISS

ANNA STANISZEWSKI

sourcebooks
jabberwocky

Published by Sourcebooks Jabberwocky, an imprint of Sourcebooks, Inc.
P.O. Box 4410, Naperville, Illinois 60567-4410
(630) 961-3900
Fax: (630) 961-2168
www.sourcebooks.com

Staniszewski, Anna.
  I'm with Cupid / Anna Staniszewski.
    pages cm. -- (Switched at first kiss ; 1)
  Summary: "When thirteen-year-olds Marcus, a supernatural matchmaker, and Lena Perris, a soul collector, kiss at a party on a dare, they soon realize their powers have swapped. Now logical-minded Lena finds herself with the love touch, and ultra-emotional Marcus has death at his fingertips--and setting things right has become a matter of love and death"-- Provided by publisher.
  [1. Supernatural--Fiction. 2. Love--Fiction. 3. Death--Fiction.] I. Title. II. Title: I am with Cupid.
  PZ7.S78685Im 2015
  [Fic]--dc23
                              2014049990

Source of Production: Versa Press, East Peoria, Illinois, USA
Date of Production: May 2015
Run Number: 5003957

Printed and bound in the United States of America.
VP 10 9 8 7 6 5 4 3 2 1

For Ray, my perfect match.

⫸━ prologue ➔

The mess all started with a kiss. Or, really, with a dare.

It was the first party of the year, and most of the eighth grade was in attendance. Lena was hovering near a bowl of Cheetos, counting the uncomfortable seconds until her friends came back from the bathroom. How long did it take to fix a "glitter emergency" anyway?

She noticed Marcus Torelli giving her a shy smile from near the Ping-Pong table. For a second, Lena considered going to talk to him. After all, they'd had fun doing their math project together last spring. But then she spotted the ratty book in his hands and glanced down at her feet instead. Someone who brought reading material to a party clearly wasn't interested in being social.

Suddenly, Connie Reynolds clapped her hands and called out, "All right, everybody! It's time to play Dare or Dare." She laughed as her guests gave her blank looks. "The 'truth' part of the game is a total waste of time," she explained before scanning the crowd, looking for her first victim. When she spotted Marcus, Connie smiled. "You! I dare you to kiss Lena Perris for five seconds."

Lena swallowed a Cheeto and whirled around to find Marcus staring back at her in horror.

"You want us to *what*?" Marcus asked. He shoved the book into his pocket and took a step toward the door. Lena wondered if he was going to make a run for it.

"Do it!" Connie said. "Or I'll make you both lick the toilet."

A chorus of "oohs" echoed through the room. Choosing toilet licking was social suicide, but saying no to Connie Reynolds was even worse.

Lena hesitated. She'd planned for her first kiss to be with Brent Adamson because of his plump lips. Marcus was nice enough and even kind of cute, but his nose was a little big. What if it got in the way?

"Remember, five seconds!" Connie squawked as she pushed Lena and Marcus toward a closet.

Then she shut the door, and they were alone.

Lena firmly planted her feet for balance and closed her eyes tight. Everything she'd read had said your eyes could *not* be open during your first kiss.

Meanwhile, Marcus's head swam at the thought of kissing Lena. He'd come to the party determined to ask her out—something he regretted not doing during their math project last year—but so far he'd spent the whole party hiding behind the Ping-Pong table. And now, here he was, alone in a closet with Lena, his lips only inches away from hers.

"So...do you want to...?" Marcus asked. His brain was screaming at him to flee before things got even more embarrassing.

"Okay," she said softly.

Marcus sucked in a breath, closed his eyes, and tipped his face forward.

At first they bumped noses. Then they bumped chins. And the third time, for some reason, it felt like they bumped ears. But finally, their lips found each other. And then—

Wow, Marcus thought as a bolt of energy zinged from the top of his skull to the bottoms of his heels. When their lips broke apart, the air around them felt charged with electricity. For a second, Marcus even thought he saw glowing wisps of smoke coming out of his shoes.

Then someone threw open the door, and it was over.

"Well, how was it?" Connie asked.

Marcus glanced at Lena and found her smiling back at him. Neither of them said a word. Seeing the end of her fun, Connie lasered in on someone else in the crowd. "Nick! I dare you to kiss Brittany!"

Marcus and Lena wandered through the party, their hands almost touching.

Something felt different. Lena thought it was the fact that she'd finally been kissed. Marcus thought it was the fact that his crush on Lena had finally turned into something more.

Of course, they were both wrong.

chapter 1

Earlier that day

Marcus stopped in front of the movie theater, patting the book in his back pocket again to make sure it was safe. The dating guide that his grandpa had given him was from the 1950s, its pages yellowed and crackling. Normally, Marcus kept it tucked away in his desk, but he'd wanted to have it with him for luck at the party tonight.

He definitely needed luck if he was finally going to ask Lena Perris out. He'd heard Lena talking to her friends about Connie Reynolds's party in the hall yesterday. Going to a party alone was loser territory, but since Marcus's best (and only) friend Pradeep had moved back to India with his family over the summer, he didn't have much of a choice. If he could finally get up the courage to ask Lena out, it would be worth the risk of adding to his awkward, shy kid reputation.

But first, he had a job to do.

He went inside the old theater, the kind with lumpy seats and tiny screens that didn't even show 3-D movies. The smell of buttery popcorn made a memory pop up in Marcus's mind: his dad bringing Marcus and his sister to see the latest Disney movie, the three of them laughing and chucking popcorn into each other's mouths. This was before his sister had turned into the perfect daughter and Marcus had turned out to be a disappointment of a son.

He shook the flood of images out of his head and scanned the lobby. After a minute, he spotted his target behind the concession stand without having to double-check the message on his phone. Christopher Costa, age 18. There was something about the teenage boy's slumped shoulders and serious eyes that told Marcus he could use his help. The flash of a faint grayish aura around his head that only Marcus could see confirmed it. For a second, Marcus could even feel how lonely the guy was.

As he watched Christopher fill up a fountain drink bigger than his own head, Marcus glanced around, trying to figure out who his target might be matched with. When he spotted the blond girl working on the other end of the concession stand, he instantly knew it was her. Even though she was a little younger and bubblier than Christopher, she looked perfect for him.

At that moment, Christopher seemed to notice Marcus lurking near the counter. "What can I get you?" he asked.

Marcus jumped. He hadn't been prepared to actually talk to his target. He was usually good at blending into the background, which was probably why none of his other assignments had even noticed him.

"Um, jelly beans," he said finally. Then he found himself explaining, "They're my grandpa's favorite."

"Oh, you're here with your grandfather?" the blond girl asked, coming up beside Christopher to grab some napkins. "That's sweet."

Marcus swallowed. "N-no. Actually, he's been in a nursing home the past few weeks, and I haven't seen him because, well…" Luckily, before he managed to spill his entire life story to complete strangers, Marcus's phone started buzzing in his pocket, telling him it was time.

He glanced around, making sure no one else was nearby, even though the manual said that when he was "on the job," people wouldn't really notice him. Sure enough, Christopher seemed to have forgotten Marcus was there. He'd dropped the jelly beans on the counter and was staring off into space like he was trying to remember something.

Marcus called up his energy, and his fingers flared a bright-red color. This was his fifth assignment, but he still expected the light to burn his fingers. Instead, all he felt was a warm tingle.

Just as Christopher started to turn away, Marcus reached

out his glowing hand and brushed the boy's arm, willing the energy to flow out of his fingers.

The moment the red light vanished, Marcus pulled his hand away, feeling dizzy. He watched Christopher stand frozen for a second and then blink a few times and glance toward the end of the counter. When his eyes met the blond girl's, the change was instantaneous.

"Hey," Christopher said, still gazing at her.

"Hey," the girl answered, taking a step toward him.

Marcus grinned as the sparks flared between them, bits of glowing dust that only he could see. His job was to give couples the initial spark—making it grow into something more was up to them—but Marcus had a good feeling about this match.

He wanted to stick around to see what would happen next, but now that his assignment was done, it was time to head to Connie Reynolds's party. He left the money for the jelly beans on the counter and hurried away. If all went well, pretty soon he'd be busy with a love match of his own.

Lena stopped her bike in front of the hospital and reread the info her boss had sent her: Odessa Albright, age 94. Whitmore Hospital, Room 301. 7:26 p.m.

She had a half hour to do her assignment and go over to

Connie Reynolds's party to meet up with her friends. Even though social gatherings weren't really her thing, Lena was actually excited about the party. Finally, she might have a chance to mark something off her "Things to Accomplish Before I Turn Fourteen" checklist.

After locking up her bike, Lena went through the hospital's revolving door and headed to the elevator. Her phone beeped as she pushed the button for the third floor. It was a message from her best friend Abigail: What are you wearing to the party?

Lena glanced down at her faded T-shirt and jeans. Should she have put more effort into her outfit if she wanted Brent Adamson to finally notice her—not to mention *kiss* her? She sighed. It was too late now.

She quickly wrote back: Same old. You?

The elevator opened, and Lena went down the hallway, searching for the right room. She knew most people hated hospitals, but she found them oddly calming. They were quiet and safe, and even though they were full of sick people, they were also bustling with doctors and nurses who were doing their best to make things right.

At room 301, she stopped and peered inside. An ancient-looking woman was asleep in the bed, a chorus of machines chiming around her. She was alone, but Lena could see dozens of bouquets and cards that people had brought her. Clearly,

Odessa Albright had had a long life filled with family and friends. And now, it was time for her to move on.

Lena's phone beeped again. I'm wearing a dress, Abigail had written back. Is that too fancy? Help!

Lena smiled and put her phone away before she went into the room. As she approached the bed, she was relieved to see that the old woman was asleep like Lena's other three collections had been.

A soft alarm on her phone went off, telling Lena it was time. She took a deep breath and then called up her energy. Almost instantly, her fingers flared with a deep-purple light. She focused on the woman's soul. After a moment, she could actually see it, a pinprick of light that glowed like late-afternoon sunshine. When she touched the woman's frail arm, the energy flowed out of Lena's hand and disappeared. Instantly, a sense of relief flooded through her, as if the soul was glad to finally be able to let go and move on to…wherever it was that souls went.

Lena pulled her hand away, feeling light-headed like she always did after a collection. She backed toward the door, knowing she only had two minutes before the woman "expired." Her boss had assured Lena that she would never have to witness death if she didn't want to.

As she hurried out of the room, still feeling drained, a hint of sadness poked at Lena's heart. But she pushed it away. Death was a downer, but it was part of life. Before she'd left, Lena's mom had been a hospice worker, so she'd taught Lena about the different stages of dying and grief and all the other things that most people didn't dare talk to their kids about.

Lena's phone beeped again. Another message from Abigail.

Hayleigh says no one will notice what I'm wearing if I put on enough glitter.

No glitter! Lena wrote back, chuckling to herself. Last time their friend Hayleigh had glittered herself from head to toe, she'd left a sparkly trail all over Lena's house. Her poor dog had had pieces of it stuck in his fur for days.

Lena hurried out of the hospital and grabbed her bike. She took a deep breath, relieved that her job was over. Now it was time to focus on the fun part of her night and her mission of finally being kissed.

She was positive that her first kiss was going to change everything.

chapter 2

The morning after the party, Lena woke up with triumph practically bursting out of her chest. She'd kissed a boy! And a whole four weeks before the deadline she'd set for herself. At this rate, she'd check off all her eighth-grade goals (first date, first kiss, first dance) by Thanksgiving.

As she jumped out of bed, Lena vowed to make Abigail a thank-you present. Maybe she'd sew her a quilted makeup bag. Lena hadn't wanted to stay at the party last night after she'd found out Brent Adamson and his plump lips weren't going to be there, but Abigail had insisted she stick around. And it had been worth it.

Of course, both Abigail and Hayleigh had wrinkled their foreheads when they'd found out about the kiss that had happened while they were in the bathroom. Hayleigh had even asked, "Isn't Marcus Torelli kind of a weirdo? He's got a nice smile, I guess, but his hair is too long and he's so quiet. And one time I saw him carrying an old model spaceship around during gym class. Who does that?"

Lena hadn't let her friend's comments bother her. Marcus was shy, but he wasn't any weirder than anyone else. And she liked the way his shaggy hair curled around his ears and the way his smile lit up his whole face so you couldn't help grinning back at him. Besides, the *who* of the first kiss didn't matter. All Lena cared about was the big, fat check mark on her list.

Lena grabbed a solar-system-themed calendar off her desk. She flipped it open to yesterday's date and carefully wrote "First Kiss" in red letters. She'd had the calendar since January, determined to mark all the big events in her life. She'd only had two before last night, and unfairly, they'd both happened on the same day. Last spring had been both her thirteenth birthday *and* the day Eddie had appeared to tell her she was a soul collector.

Now, finally, Lena had something else major to write down in her calendar. If all went well, on Monday she'd be able to add "made the school play" too.

She hummed to herself as she made her bed, lining up the corners of her handmade quilt so they were perfectly even. Her friends liked to tease her about her quilting hobby, but Lena didn't care. Quilts were all straight lines and predictable patterns. They made a whole lot more sense than people did.

As she finished fluffing her last pillow, Lena's phone rang. It was her boss Eduardo, a.k.a. Eddie.

"Hey, kid," he said in his faint Spanish accent. "I have another job for you this morning."

"Already? I just did one yesterday."

Eddie let out a distracted-sounding chuckle. Lena was willing to bet he was playing with some new gadget while he talked to her. Even though he was around her dad's age, Eddie was like a big kid who always had to have the latest tech toys. "It's a busy time of year. Lots of jobs in the fall."

"There's a 'busy season' for people dying?" Lena asked with a laugh.

"You would be surprised. Statistically speaking—"

On second thought, Lena didn't feel like listening to Eddie ramble on about numbers. "I know this is against the rules, but is there any way someone else could take over for me today?" she interrupted. "I'm supposed to go over to my friend's house to get ready for *Alice in Wonderland* auditions. It's really, really important."

"No can do, kid. Once a job is assigned to you, it's yours. But if you like theater, then you will enjoy this one. Be there in an hour. I'll send you the address." Before she could resort to begging, Eddie had already hung up.

Lena sighed and started getting dressed. Maybe if her job didn't take long, she could go over to Abigail's after.

A minute later, she heard her dad calling from down the hall. "Lena! Are you awake or have you developed somniloquy?"

"Somnilo-what?" she called back, opening her bedroom door.

"Talking in your sleep!" her dad answered.

When Lena shuffled into the kitchen, Professor rushed over to greet her by dropping a dirty sock at her feet. At least it was hers this time and not the next-door neighbor's.

"Thanks, boy," she said, scratching behind his pointy German shepherd ears. He rubbed up against her leg, leaving a coating of fur on her pajamas, before going back to his post at the sliding glass door that looked out onto the yard. Tracking the neighborhood's squirrel activity was Professor's favorite pastime.

Even though it was Sunday, Lena's dad was sitting at the table dressed in his work clothes, flipping through a scientific journal and sipping a mug of hot water. Once again, he'd forgotten to put coffee into the coffeemaker and was too distracted to notice how bland his "cup of joe" tasted. If he started eating air instead of toast, Lena would have to have a serious talk with him.

For a second, she had a flash of how things used to be. Dad bustling around the kitchen, making cheesy scrambled eggs for her and Mom. Mom fixing the coffee so it would be just right. Dad turning to Lena and saying something like, "Chipmunk, you're right on time!"

No. Lena squashed the memory down, down, down. That life didn't exist anymore. Really, it never had. Not when, all that time, her mom had been planning to leave.

"Lena, good, you're up," Dad said, glancing up from his magazine. He never called her Chipmunk anymore. "Have a seat. I need to talk to you."

She perched on the edge of a chair. This couldn't be a good sign. Her dad was always saying that breakfast should come before pretty much anything else.

"What's wrong? Is Mom okay?" Normally, she wouldn't ask him about such a sore topic, but thoughts of her mom were still bouncing around in her brain.

Her dad put down his mug. "As far as I know, your mother is fine. If anything happened, I'm sure your grandmother would let us know," he said in his level, scientist voice. Dad had always been pretty low on the emotional scale, but since Mom had left, he'd practically turned into a talking piece of wood.

"Then what is it?" Lena's stomach plummeted into her toes. Oh no. Had her dad found out her secret somehow?

Eddie had made Lena swear not to tell anyone about her alter ego, but even if he hadn't, Lena would *not* have shared the truth with her dad. He'd probably do a scientific study on her and publish it: *The Neurochemistry of a Teen Soul Collector*. No way. She wanted to be a famous actress, not a famous case study.

"Lena," he announced, "I have a lunch date today."

She had to laugh. "A date? Is this Aunt Teresa's doing again?"

He slowly shook his head. "I should have known better than to have dinner alone with my sister. She always manages to talk me into these dates, and then…" He took another sip of hot water.

Suddenly, something in Lena's vision changed, like someone had colored in the air around her dad with a gray marker. And for a moment, all she could think was how horribly, miserably lonely he was.

But that was crazy. Dad wasn't lonely. He was fine!

Lena blinked, and the gray color disappeared, along with the wave of sadness that had crashed over her.

"Are you all right?" her dad asked. "You look a little pale."

Whatever that weird aura had been, it was gone now. "I'm great." If she mentioned suddenly seeing gray clouds, her dad would drag her in for a brain scan or something. "So who is this woman?"

He let out a soft laugh. "She's actually a scientist too. Your aunt Teresa met her at one of her book groups. She's a physicist."

"She sounds perfect for you," Lena had to admit as she got to her feet.

"I don't want you to worry that anything will change," Dad said. "You know how I feel about romantic love."

"I know. It's only chemicals in our brains that make us think we're in love," she recited, grabbing a cereal bowl.

"Exactly. And once those chemicals fade, what are we left with? Nothing."

Since her dad studied brain chemistry, he had to know what he was talking about. His theory certainly explained how Lena's mom could have left the two of them behind. It was also why Lena had decided to work her way through a checklist of things to accomplish before she turned fourteen. She was *not* going to let hormones and brain chemicals control who she kissed or dated or danced with. She was determined to have an average middle-school experience without all the drama that usually went with it. The only drama she was interested in was the onstage kind.

"Dad?" Lena asked in between bites of granola. "I'm going over to Abigail's to run lines for *Alice* tryouts, okay?" She didn't mention that she had to make a quick stop on the way.

He nodded, still clearly distracted thinking about the horrors of dating. Then he glanced up as if he'd finally registered what she'd said. "So you're trying out again this year? Good! I like to see that kind of perseverance." How embarrassing that even her dad thought she probably wouldn't get in.

Lena's phone beeped, reminding her she had a half hour to get to the collection location.

She rushed to finish getting ready and kissed her dad good-bye. Forget the school play. It was time to go on soul patrol again.

chapter 3

As Lena rode her bike over to the address on her phone, she ran through the audition scene from *Alice* in her head. She knew better than to hope for the lead, but maybe this year, they'd at least cast her as a tree. She had to get into the play if she was ever going to make her dream—the dream she'd had since fifth grade—come true.

That spring, not long before she'd moved out, her mom had taken Lena to a Shakespeare festival. Lena had been mesmerized. For once, she hadn't thought about the "chemical reactions that caused emotional attachments" and the other things her dad was always going on about. She'd simply believed the story the actors were telling, and she'd even imagined they were performing it just for her.

After the play, she'd sworn to herself that she would be up there on that stage one day, no matter what. So far, the closest she'd gotten was backstage in the dusty wings at school.

When Lena got to Mrs. Katz's house, she jumped off her bike and stashed it behind some bushes. The front door was unlocked thanks to the science—Lena refused to think of it as magic—of soul collecting. She took a second to get herself focused and then went inside.

As Lena wandered through the house, the air thick with the smell of freshly baked gingerbread, she was expecting this assignment to be a sleeper like the others had been. That's why she sucked in a surprised breath when she spotted the old woman, Mrs. Katz, sitting at her dining room table, flipping through a stack of photo albums. Totally awake.

Eddie had warned Lena that her assignments would get harder as they went along, but she hadn't expected it to happen so soon. *Breathe*, she told herself, trying to swallow the sudden pounding in her throat. *You'll be okay.*

Lena stepped quietly through the room, although Mrs. Katz didn't seem to notice she was there, and was surprised to see that the photo albums on the table weren't full of family pictures. They were old grainy photos of actors on a fancy stage.

Something clicked in Lena's head. She'd met Mrs. Katz before. The old woman always came to the plays at Lena's school. She'd sit in the front row, and after the play, she'd come up to all the kids in the cast and tell them what a good job they'd done. Lena had always been in the wings, organizing props and lugging around sets, but she liked to think that Mrs. Katz was congratulating her too.

And now, Lena had to gather her soul.

Why did this assignment have to be somebody she knew? And why couldn't Mrs. Katz at least be asleep?

But Lena knew she had no choice. This was the order of things. This was how the world worked. She had to do it quickly, before she lost her nerve. That's why Eddie had said she'd been chosen to be a soul collector in the first place, because of her no-nonsense approach to life and death.

She planted her feet squarely under her shoulders and focused on calling up her energy. The only time her touch was actually dangerous was when her fingers were glowing and her mind was completely focused on the soul in front of her. The manual insisted that it could never happen by accident. Souls weren't willing to leave their bodies unless it was their time, and even then, they needed a soul collector's energy to set them loose so they could move on to "After."

Lena often wondered what "After" was like, but Eddie refused to talk about it. All he'd say was that, "It is a place any of us would be glad to live."

Her dad, of course, would insist that there was "little scientific probability of an afterlife, blah blah blah," but as Lena positioned herself behind Mrs. Katz, she hoped what Eddie said was true.

After a moment of total concentration, her fingers started to glow purple. Except…they weren't quite purple. They were closer to maroon. Or maybe even red. That was weird.

But Lena didn't have a chance to think it over because her phone started to beep, telling her she had two minutes to do her job and get out of there.

She closed her eyes and focused on sensing the woman's soul. Then she let the energy pulse out of her hand and into Mrs. Katz's shoulder. When it was done, Lena stepped away, her head spinning.

"I'm sorry," she whispered. "I hope you're happy wherever you're going."

As she backed out of the room, Lena watched Mrs. Katz put down the photo album and draw in a sharp breath. The old woman's body seemed to sag…

And then she sat straight up and let out a surprised-sounding laugh.

Lena stared. Huh?

Mrs. Katz jumped to her feet and laughed again. Then she did something like a jig across the room.

What was going on?

Suddenly, the doorbell rang. Oh no. This wasn't how the soul collection was supposed to go! Whoever was at the door was probably meant to discover Mrs. Katz's body.

Lena dove behind a bookcase as Mrs. Katz went down the hallway. She tried summoning energy in her hand again, but it was too late. She'd missed her window.

Mrs. Katz swung open the front door. "Hello!" she sang. "Isn't it a lovely morning?"

Lena peeked around the bookcase and saw an elderly mailman standing on the stoop, holding a small box.

"Are you Mrs. Cecelia Katz?" he asked, reading the label.

"Yes."

"I have a delivery for…" He finally looked up and met Mrs. Katz's gaze. "You."

The two of them stared at each other for so long that Lena thought maybe they were frozen. Suddenly, the weird shift in her vision happened again, like she'd put on a pair of glasses, and the air around the two old people turned bright yellow. In the lemony haze, sparks flitted between them like lightning bugs.

Lena gave her head a firm shake, trying to snap herself out of whatever this was. She didn't have time for her brain to play tricks on her. She had to *think*.

Finally, right as Lena's vision cleared, Mrs. Katz giggled and said to the mailman, "Would you like to come inside?"

Lena ducked behind the bookcase again as the two practically waltzed into the living room. She didn't know what to do. Stay and try to fix things? Leave and come back later? She couldn't remember the manual saying anything about this kind of situation.

Finally, she grabbed her phone and sent Eddie a message. Emergency! Something went wrong with the Katz assignment!

She hid in the corner, listening to Mrs. Katz and the mailman giggling over absolutely nothing. The old lady was acting like Connie Reynolds did around guys, throwing her head back and laughing so all her teeth showed. At least Connie's teeth were all real.

After ten minutes, Eddie still hadn't gotten back to her. Maybe he was trying out a new video game or something. In that case, it could be hours before he called her back. Lena had to get out of here. She'd never seen old people flirting before. It was scarier than watching a horror movie.

She'd come back later, she decided, after she'd heard from Eddie about how to fix this.

Lena slipped outside and got back on her bike. As she pedaled home, dripping with sweat, her mind whirled. What had gone wrong? She'd done everything by the book. Yes, Mrs. Katz was the first awake person she'd been assigned, but that shouldn't matter, should it? Once she was home, she'd go through the manual and see if there was something there that could explain what had happened.

Her phone beeped. Lena pulled over, hoping it was Eddie. No such luck. It was Abigail, wondering when she was coming over. Running lines was the last thing on Lena's mind right now, but how could she explain to Abigail that something had come up that was literally a matter of life and death? Instead, she told her friend she was sick and started pedaling for home again.

Think, she told herself. Something had to be different. Well, there had been that red light coming out of her fingers. *That* had never happened before.

Lena hit the brakes. That had to be it. But what did it mean? She'd collected four souls before today, and her energy had always been purple. She hadn't eaten anything strange or accidentally stepped in radioactive goo. Just in case, she checked the bottoms of her sneakers. Nothing.

Her phone beeped. Sick? Abigail had written back. See? I told you you shouldn't have kissed Marcus Torelli! You probably got his germs.

Her first kiss.

That was something different. After all, the whole point of rites of passage was that your life was never supposed to be the same again. And then she remembered the energy that had raced through her when her lips had touched Marcus's and how the air had seemed to crackle around them. For a second, she'd even thought she'd seen weird smoke coming out of her shoes. Maybe that hadn't just been a chemical reaction to a first kiss. Maybe that had been something else.

But why would her power get messed up because of a kiss? Had some of it rubbed off on Marcus and that's why it wasn't working the right way?

No, Lena told herself. Marcus had seemed totally fine when she'd left the party last night. If her power had somehow affected him, she would have seen it right away.

Still, she should check on him, just in case. Maybe that would help her figure out what had gone wrong.

Her heart clanging in her chest, Lena changed direction and started pedaling furiously toward Marcus's house.

chapter 4

Before he'd become a supernatural matchmaker, Marcus had spent his whole life being not enough. Not brave enough, not smart enough, and certainly not strong enough. Nothing like his perfect, fearless sister. The only thing he'd ever been decent at was fixing old model spaceships, but according to Marcus's dad, that hobby was nothing but a "royal waste of time."

Then, on his thirteenth birthday, Marcus had finally discovered something he was just right at. Of course, it was a shame he couldn't tell anyone—not even Grandpa Joe—about being a matchmaker, but his boss Eddie's reassurances that he was a natural were good enough.

Or at least they had been.

Now, Marcus couldn't stop thinking about Lena and what she would say if he told her the truth. For some reason, he thought she might understand.

As he sat at his desk trying to focus on his homework, last

night's kiss played over and over in his head. He couldn't believe how easily it had all happened.

He glanced at the book that Grandpa Joe had given him last month before he had to move into the nursing home: *How to Win the Girl of Your Dreams*. Even though it was faded and musty and used words like "swell" and "boss," Grandpa swore by that book. "Thanks to this little thing," he'd said, "I got your grandma to marry me!"

Marcus figured if the moldy guide had helped his grandparents find each other and stay together for over forty years, then it had to help him finally get Lena to like him. Maybe then he wouldn't chicken out every time he thought of asking her out.

But the book wasn't much help at the moment. According to its crackling pages, you were never supposed to kiss a girl on a first date. Last night hadn't even been a date, so now what?

Should he call her? Text her? Show up at her house? The thought of doing any of that stuff made his stomach shudder, but he couldn't wimp out, not when things were finally going right.

He flipped through the book for what felt like the hundredth time. *Don't be too eager*, it reminded him in its friendly font. "When you see her, always bring flowers." Bingo. He'd wait until tomorrow and bring her some roses from his sister's garden. (On top of all her other annoying accomplishments, Ann-Marie managed to grow the biggest rosebushes in town.)

That settled, Marcus finally gave up on his homework and went over to his worktable, where his latest project—a vintage moon ship he and Grandpa Joe had found at a yard sale—was waiting. He'd had to slowly take the model apart to figure out which pieces were missing and then start to put it back together again. There were still a couple of parts he hadn't been able to find, but he was sure he'd track them down. Then he'd reassemble the pieces, touch up the paint, and the ship would be whole again. Maybe once it was done, he'd finally work up the courage to go to the nursing home to show Grandpa Joe the finished product. Since it was identical to a model that Grandpa had had growing up, Marcus knew he'd get a kick out of seeing it restored.

Marcus's phone rang, pulling him out of his thoughts. He put down his tools and said "Hey, Eddie" without checking to see who it was. Now that Pradeep lived in a whole other country, no one else ever called. "Got another assignment for me?"

"You got it, kid," said Eddie. "I wish all my employees were as excited as you. I will send the details in a minute."

"I checked on the couple from my assignment last month, and I could still see a spark between them. I think they're going to last."

"You did a good job with that one," Eddie said with a distracted chuckle. "What is that? Four out of four?"

"If you count yesterday's, five for five," Marcus said, his chest filling with pride.

As long as the couple from the movie theater stayed together, he'd be the first matchmaker to have so many successful matches out of the gate. That was a pretty big deal, considering that they'd only lowered the matchmaking age to thirteen a few years ago.

"Of course a hopeless romantic like you is a natural," Eddie said. "That must be why you already see auras. I did not see my first one until I was a young man of nineteen, and I had already done dozens of matches by then."

"Wait, you used to do matches?" Marcus asked. For some reason, he'd assumed Eddie had always been a middleman.

"Oh, yes," Eddie said, his voice growing quiet. "I did for a while, before I got this job."

"So if I keep doing well, one day I'll get promoted to a manager like you were?" He had never met a fellow matchmaker, and Eddie didn't like to say too much about "the network," but Marcus was dying to know how it all worked.

Eddie coughed. "Listen, kid. You should probably get going or you will miss your match." Then, before Marcus could say anything else, he hung up.

Marcus stared at his phone for a minute, trying to figure what he'd said wrong. He'd never asked Eddie about his past before, but it was clearly a sore topic. He wanted to apologize, but he had no idea what to apologize *for*. Sadly, a lot of the conversations he had with people ended that way. If only he'd inherited Grandpa Joe's talent for talking to people and making them laugh. Instead, he'd only managed to figure out how to get people to laugh at him.

Marcus sighed and threw open his bedroom door. He almost tripped over his sister, who was doing some kind of weird stretch in the middle of the hallway, one foot up on each wall.

"Hey!" Ann-Marie said. "Watch it!"

"Can't you do that in the basement?"

"No," she said, huffing. "Dad gave me some new stretches, and he said this one should be done in a hallway. Besides, Mom's working on another trash sculpture downstairs. It reeks." She looked past him. "Ew! Do you still have that gross terrarium on your desk? That turtle died, like, a month ago!"

"So?" He quickly shut his bedroom door behind him.

Ann-Marie snorted. "Are you gonna cry all over again if you have to get rid of it?"

Marcus felt his cheeks go hot. The worst moment of his life had been seeing George, the turtle he'd had since he was a little kid, lying lifeless in the corner of the terrarium. The second worst moment of his life had been a minute later when his parents and sister had witnessed him bursting into tears. His dad had barely looked at him for days. After all, Ann-Marie had broken her toe during a track meet last year and still managed to win her race, all without shedding a single tear.

He picked his way through the hallway, weaving around the free weights and exercise mats his dad was always bringing home for Ann-Marie to try out. When Marcus went past the living room, he noticed that two more medals had appeared on the mantel, meaning the last visible family photo with Marcus in it was now covered up.

As he passed a rowing machine near the couch, he gave its leg a frustrated kick. No wonder he couldn't make any new friends. How was he supposed to invite anyone over when his mom's weird eco-sculptures were always smelling up the house and his dad had turned the living room into a cross between a gym and a shrine to all his sister's accomplishments?

His phone beeped. Half an hour to get to the park. Marcus grabbed a piece of cold pizza from the fridge and inhaled it, then washed it down with some orange juice.

"Where are Mom and Dad?" he called to his sister.

Ann-Marie let out a groan that probably meant she was contorting herself into some ever-weirder stretch. "Visiting Grandpa again before Dad takes me to the track later. Are you ever gonna go with them?"

Marcus coughed. "What? Yeah. I'm busy, that's all." His

mom had assured him that Grandpa Joe was going to be okay after the heart attack he'd had a few weeks ago, but Marcus had been avoiding visiting him. The thought of Grandpa in some all-beige nursing home like the ones on TV, surrounded by old people who didn't even know their own names, was unbearable. Grandpa didn't belong in a place like that. "Tell them I went to the park, okay?"

"Since when do you like nature?" Ann-Marie asked.

"I have to, um, study some leaves for a project." Marcus tried to base his lies as much on the truth as possible so he didn't get caught. Still, making up excuses seemed to get harder every time he had an assignment.

"Leaves?" his sister asked, finally sitting up. Her face was flushed from being upside down for so long. "I don't remember a project like that."

"Yeah, it's for science. It's new."

She tugged her hair out of its ponytail and cornered him. "I'm so glad I'm in high school. We don't have to do dumb stuff like that anymore. In my honors English class, we're..."

And then something strange happened. As Ann-Marie went on about how interesting and challenging and amazing all her classes were, for a moment, Marcus saw a blindingly bright light shining from inside her. It made her whole chest light up as if she had a lamp lodged in her rib cage.

"Um, Ann-Marie?" Marcus asked. "Are you okay?"

She didn't seem to hear him as she babbled on about her English project. And then, as suddenly as it had appeared, the light started to fade. Marcus blinked, still seeing the outline of it on the backs of his eyelids. And then it was gone.

What on earth was that? He'd seen auras when he was matchmaking, but those only showed up when he was looking at people who were assigned to him. And this hadn't been a hazy outline around someone's head. This had been something else.

But then Marcus's phone buzzed, reminding him that he was running out of time to get to the park. As he dodged around his sister and rushed out the door, he temporarily forgot all about the strange light he'd seen.

chapter 5

Marcus was panting by the time he got to the end of his street. He was going to have to run all the way to the park to avoid being late. And that was only if he got past Caspar Brown's house without a problem. If he missed his assignment, well...Marcus wasn't sure exactly what would happen, but Eddie was always talking about "maintaining the balance of the universe." If a couple wasn't matched when it was supposed to be, that couldn't be good for the balance of anything.

As he rounded the corner, Marcus held his breath, praying Caspar wouldn't be outside. His stomach sank when, sure enough, he spotted an ape-shaped boy in the middle of the street. In true simian style, Caspar was hurling rocks into a nearby pond.

Marcus froze in his tracks. Should he turn around and go the long way instead? If he ran at full speed, maybe he could still make it to the park on time. At least Caspar hadn't see him—

"Hey, Marcus! Come over here!"

No no no no no!

Marcus spun around, trying to flee, but Caspar was on him in an instant. "Where are you going?" he asked, grabbing his shoulder with a meaty paw.

"I-I've gotta go," Marcus stammered. "I'm late."

"I don't see you around anymore. And what happened to your sidekick? Did he get shipped off to nerd camp?"

"He moved," Marcus said, wishing Pradeep were here with him now. His friend would have made a goofy joke and lightened the mood so Caspar would let them go. Now Marcus was on his own.

His phone buzzed. Ten minutes until the match. "I really have to go," he said, trying to wriggle out from under Caspar's enormous grasp. The two of them were in the same grade, but Marcus was convinced that Caspar had been held back in kindergarten—probably twice. How else could he be so much bigger than everyone else?

Caspar didn't let go. Instead, he yanked the phone from Marcus's hand and sneered at it. "Where'd you get this piece of junk? Did your mom find it in a landfill?"

"Give it back—"

"I saw her Dumpster diving behind the school last week. What are you guys, homeless or something?"

Heat flared in Marcus's chest, like someone had lit a torch in his lungs. "She's an artist," he said through clenched teeth. "She uses that stuff in her sculptures." He took a step forward and tried to snatch his phone back, but it was too late.

Caspar's lips stretched into a grin as he wound his arm back and flung the phone toward the pond. It landed in the mosquito-infested water with a soul-crushing *plop*.

Marcus stared. Oh God. His phone. It was his only way of contacting Eddie.

He realized that Caspar had finally let go of his arm, so he scrambled over to the edge of the pond. He could make out the shape of the phone on the bottom, like a rectangular pebble.

"You gonna go diving for trash like your mom does?" Caspar called.

Marcus wanted to punch him. He wanted to jump into the water, grab the phone, and throw it in Caspar's face. Instead, he took one more look at his ruined phone and turned away. Then he ran as fast as he could.

By the time Marcus got to the park, he was gasping for breath and his entire body was shaking. He couldn't tell if the shaking was from exhaustion or rage. If he missed his match on top of everything that had happened…

No. He was going to make it. He didn't know why he was so certain, but he knew that he still had another minute.

Even though he couldn't double-check the info on his phone, he spotted his target right away: a young woman with short dreadlocks and a nose ring, her face framed by oval glasses. Olivia Monroe, age 26. The way she sat on the park bench slowly untying and retying her running shoes told him that she needed a "love boost," as the manual called it. He squinted, searching for the grayish aura that normally hovered around his targets and the feeling of loneliness that usually went with it, but nothing changed. That didn't matter. Marcus was sure it was her.

As he got closer though, he realized that without his phone, he wouldn't know the exact time to zap Olivia. He had no idea who she was going to be matched with—maybe the guy eating a bagel on a nearby bench or the tall woman across the street— but if he didn't make the connection at the right moment, he'd miss his window. He'd have to try to do it by feel.

Marcus took a shaky breath and concentrated on getting the spark into his fingers. It flared almost right away, much more quickly than it had the other times. For some reason, it was darker in color than normal. Closer to purple than red. Maybe that meant his matchmaking powers were getting stronger. Good! The more powerful that first jolt, the more time the two people had to get to know each other before the spark wore off. That would definitely keep his success rate high.

He stood there for a second, breathing everything in. He knew somehow that the moment was almost right. He moved his hand into position behind Olivia's shoulder and—

BAM!

Something smashed into his chest and sent him sailing back through the air. His hand barely grazed Olivia's neck before he fell to the ground. And then everything went dark.

chapter 6

Someone was on top of him, yelling words he couldn't understand.

Marcus's head swam, and it was hard to focus. He vaguely registered that he'd fallen onto the grass and that he must have hit his head pretty hard. But why was some crazy person pinning him to the ground?

Finally, his eyes cleared, and he recognized her. Lena Perris.

He had to be seeing things. Why would Lena be here? And why would she be sitting on top of him and screaming?

"Marcus!" she was shouting, her words coming to him through a fog. The voice really did sound like Lena's. Maybe it *was* her. "Did you touch her? Did you?"

He didn't know what she was talking about. For some reason, all he could think about was the book his grandpa had given him. *Always pay the girl a compliment*, it said.

"You look nice today," he told her.

Lena let out a cry of frustration. Then she jumped up, leaving him sprawled on the ground.

As Marcus finally pulled himself together and sat up on the grass, he remembered Olivia. He'd missed his window to zap her! Or had he? He'd felt at least some of the energy leave his fingers before Lena had knocked him over.

When he looked toward the bench, Lena was leaning over someone else who was on the ground. Was she going around tackling *everyone*?

As Marcus got to his feet, his head pounding, he realized that it was Olivia who was spread out on the grass by the bench. Her eyes were closed, and she wasn't moving.

"You!" Lena cried, pointing to a redheaded man who was jogging by. "Call 911!"

The man stopped and stared down at Olivia. Then he nodded urgently, pulled out his phone, and started dialing.

That's when it finally clicked for Marcus that something was wrong. He ran over and knelt beside Olivia. She was breathing, but her breaths seemed small and shallow.

Lena was checking the woman's airways and pulse like they'd learned during first aid last year. Since she didn't start CPR, he thought maybe that was a good sign.

"Is she okay? What happened to her?" he asked.

"You almost killed her," Lena said softly.

Marcus couldn't help it. He laughed. "What are you talking about?"

Lena shook her head. "I'm not sure why, but somehow things got mixed up." She glanced at the people gathering around to see if the woman was okay. The redheaded guy was hovering over them, still holding his phone. "I shouldn't be talking about this here. I shouldn't be talking about this at all!"

"Talking about what?" Marcus asked, but at that moment, the ambulance pulled up. After that, everything was a blur of flashing lights and stretchers and IVs. It made Marcus think of his grandpa. Is this what things had been like after he'd collapsed at home a few weeks ago?

"Marcus?" he heard Lena say.

He blinked, realizing that the ambulance was pulling away. No one had asked him what had happened. Lena must have done all the talking.

"I still don't understand what's going on," he said.

"Come on," Lena said as she led him to a nearby bench. "I have to tell you something. This is going to sound crazy, and it's against the rules for me to even *think* about telling you this, but you need to know or you might hurt someone else." She peered down at her sneakers, as if she were trying to find the right words in her shoelaces. "The thing is, I'm a soul collector. And I think somehow you got my powers. When we, you know…when we kissed last night."

Marcus stared at her. "A soul collector?"

"I know what you're thinking, but I'm not the grim reaper or anything like that. See? No hood or pointy gardening tool. And I don't kill anyone, but I do have the power to draw souls out of people's bodies and send them to…wherever they go. Only I think you have my power now. Or at least part of it."

All he could do was stare at her, oddly focused on her slightly crooked front teeth.

"When I realized something was wrong," she went on, "I stopped by your house, and your sister said you were here. I rode my bike over as fast as I could, but I don't know if it was in time. You…you almost pulled that woman's soul out of her body."

He should have been shocked at the idea of someone being able to take souls, especially someone like Lena. But if he could make people fall in love with a bolt of energy, then why couldn't those other things be true? Still…people didn't just swap powers. He'd memorized the manual Eddie had given him, and nowhere did it even hint at anything like that being possible.

He wanted to tell Lena all this, but instead he found himself saying, "It's a scythe."

She blinked. "What?"

"The scary pointy tool. It's called a scythe. And it's for farming, not gardening. I read about it in a book on the history of—"

"You're not getting the point. You almost killed someone!" Lena cried, nostrils flaring. "I'm not saying it's your fault, but didn't you notice that something was wrong? Didn't you think it was kind of weird that your fingers were glowing?"

"Not exactly—" Marcus began, but she wasn't listening.

"Whatever is going on, I need to figure out how to fix it." Lena pulled out her phone. "I'll try sending Eddie another message. Why is he ignoring me when I told him it was an emergency?"

"Eddie?" Marcus repeated.

"Yes," she said, furiously typing on her phone. "He's my boss."

"Wait. Eddie's your boss?" Marcus couldn't believe it. Was there a staffing shortage or something? "Eddie's my boss too."

She didn't look up. "That's nice."

"No, you don't get it. Eduardo? Grayish hair, dark beard? Sounds like he lived in Spain a million years ago? Loves gadgets?"

Lena looked up, her eyes suddenly suspicious. "How do you know all that?"

"I'm telling you. He's my boss too. You're a soul collector? Well, I'm a matchmaker. Like Cupid but without the diaper."

Before she could answer, someone behind them let out a loud whistle. An instant later, Eddie sped around the corner on a Segway. He was exactly as Marcus had described him.

"Well, shoot," Eddie said when he'd pulled up in front of them. "So you two really did swap powers. How are we going to fix that?"

chapter 7

L ena's brain felt like it was about to explode. Marcus was some kind of supernatural matchmaker? If she didn't have Eddie standing two feet away, confirming the fact that it was true, she would have laughed right in his face. Being a soul collector was one thing. Death was a normal part of life. But love? Love was a total lie invented by the people who made romantic comedies and heart-shaped candy. Just ask her dad about that.

"This is crazy," she said, jumping to her feet. "How is it possible to switch powers?"

Eddie shook his head, still perched on his Segway, his red helmet gleaming in the sun. "It should not be, but somehow it has happened. At least, that is the message I got. And my boss is *not* happy. So give me the details."

"Wait, what about Olivia?" Marcus asked. "Is she going to be okay?"

Lena figured that had to be the woman he'd zapped.

Eddie waved his hand dismissively, sending his Segway wobbling. "Don't worry about that right now. Just tell me when you first knew something was wrong."

"It was during my collection," Lena said. "I zapped Mrs. Katz like I was supposed to, but instead of dying, she got all weird and started giggling with the mailman."

"The mailman?" Marcus let out a weak laugh. "Maybe he'll send her love letters." Clearly, the whole situation was too much for him to handle.

"Wait," Lena said, her brain finally starting to process what Marcus had told her. "That happened because of *your* powers, didn't it? I made those old people think they're in love."

Marcus stared at her. "They don't just think it. They *are* in love. At least for now. Once it starts to fade, they'll have to—"

"Back up," Eddie broke in. "Do you have any idea what caused this?"

"I'm pretty sure it was the kiss," Lena said. She glanced at Marcus to see if he agreed and saw his cheeks go pink. Was he seriously going to get embarrassed about their kiss when he'd almost killed someone?

"We were at a party last night," she went on, "and Connie Reynolds dared us to kiss. So we did it, and then today, everything's all messed up."

"A kiss?" Eddie asked, scratching his short beard. "What did it feel like, exactly?"

Lena thought back, replaying the moment in her mind. "Electric, I guess. It was…"

"It was amazing," Marcus chimed in. Then his cheeks grew an even darker shade of pink, like two wads of cotton candy.

"Electricity?" Eddie asked thoughtfully. "That might have something to do with it. I mean, your powers are both fueled by energy. It makes sense that when that energy meets, it would spark. Like wires accidently getting crossed."

"So what do we do to uncross them?" asked Lena.

Eddie smiled, looking relieved. "Well, kid, that's pretty obvious, isn't it? You two need to kiss again. That should fix everything."

Lena glanced at Marcus, who seemed like he might pass out. "Here?" she asked. The crowd had drifted away after the ambulance had left, but she didn't exactly want to kiss a boy in the middle of a park with her boss watching. She was pretty sure that particular "teen first" wasn't listed in any of the magazines she'd read.

"Come on, kids," said Eddie. "The faster we undo this, the better. I cannot be on probation again."

"Probation?" Lena asked, but Eddie was clapping his hands insistently like they didn't have another second to lose. "Fine."

She jumped up, eager to get this over with. She'd given up on running lines with Abigail today, but at least she could go back home and look over the audition piece after this whole crazy thing was fixed.

Marcus got to his feet and took a few cautious steps toward her. Finally, they were face-to-face again. This was nothing like the closet last night. For one thing, they hadn't had someone staring right at them last time.

"Um, Eddie?" Lena said. "Can you look away or something?"

He shrugged and spun his wheels around so his back was turned.

"Okay," she said. "On the count of three. One. Two. Three."

They both rushed their faces forward and—*thunk!*—bumped foreheads.

"Ow!" Marcus cried, rubbing his temples.

"Sorry!" said Lena. "Are you okay?"

"Sounds like you're doing it wrong," Eddie called over his shoulder.

Lena sighed and took a step forward. "Let's try it slower this time." She focused on his eyes and realized, suddenly, what an unusual shade of brown they were. In the sunlight, they almost looked like the pieces of amber in a necklace her mom had once had.

"What?" Marcus asked.

Lena blinked. "Um, nothing. It's...your eyes." For some reason, her face started to feel hot.

"Well?" Eddie called to them.

"We're trying!" Marcus said. Then he gave Lena a determined look and started to inch his face toward hers. When he was only a whisper away, Lena closed her eyes. Finally, their lips met and...

Nothing. Absolutely nothing. She might as well have been kissing a watermelon.

She pulled away, studying Marcus's expression for any sign that he'd felt something, but his cheeks were the same shade of pink as before.

"Well?" Eddie called again.

"You can turn around now," Lena said.

"Good," he said, cruising over. "Now, let's see if that worked. Call up your energy, both of you."

Lena took a deep breath and summoned her energy. It took more effort than normal, but finally her fingers started to glow. She sighed as she saw they were still the wrong color. Meanwhile, Marcus's were the exact shade of purple that hers should have been.

"Still nothing," Eddie said, and Lena couldn't help noticing how worried he sounded.

"Should we...should we kiss again?" Marcus asked.

But Eddie was shaking his head. "This doesn't make sense. The kiss should have fixed it. Are you sure you did everything the same way?"

"Well, there was the party and everything," said Lena. "And we were in a closet."

"A closet?" Eddie seemed to think this over. "Okay, follow me." He zipped across the park to a tiny shack where the bathrooms were. On the side of the building was a door that looked like it led to a storage room. He hopped off the Segway and tried to open the door, but the handle wouldn't budge. Eddie started whistling tunelessly to himself as he took out some kind of gadget that looked like an oversized Swiss army knife. He inserted one end into the lock and—*click!*—it opened.

He turned and gave Lena and Marcus a devilish grin. "Shh, you never saw me with this," he said, tucking the contraption back into his pocket. "Okay, in you go."

Lena peered into the tiny room full of cleaning supplies and dented trash barrels. "In there?"

"You wanted a closet? I found you a closet. Now, let's go. The boss lady will be calling me any minute, and I want to be able to tell her the crisis is over."

"Come on," Marcus said, heading inside. "Let's give it a try."

Lena sighed and followed him. If this was how disastrous

her rites of passage were going to be, she wasn't sure she wanted to do them anymore.

When Lena and Marcus were inside, half-choked by the smells of dirt and bleach, Eddie slammed the door shut, and they were alone in the darkness.

"This is pretty crazy, huh?" Marcus said after a minute.

"That's a total understatement. Let's get this over with." Lena heard him suck in a breath and realized how harsh her words must have sounded. "Sorry," she added more softly. "This is just all so crazy. I woke up really happy this morning and now…"

"I know," he said. "But it'll be okay. We'll fix it."

She let out a long breath and took a step forward. This time, even though the light was dim, their lips managed to find each other right away. Maybe they were getting better at this whole kissing thing.

Lena closed her eyes and waited for the *zing* to charge through her body again.

Nothing.

Marcus pulled away first this time. "I don't get it. I mean… it was nice." He let out an embarrassed chuckle. "Really nice. But it's not the same."

"I know!" She focused on her fingers, and a moment later, they sparked red again. "It didn't work."

Just then, Eddie threw open the door. "Well, how was it?" he asked, sounding eerily like Connie Reynolds.

The two of them shook their heads, and Eddie's face fell. "Shoot," he said. "This is not good. It should have worked!"

Lena had never heard Eddie sound so stressed out before, and judging by the frown on Marcus's face, he hadn't either. "Um, Eddie?" she asked. "You *can* fix this, can't you?"

"I am doing the best I can!" he barked. Then he cleared his throat and gave her a forced smile. "Okay. You two just sit tight until I can find the answer."

"Sit tight?" Lena cried. "I'm a *cupid*!"

"Matchmaker," Marcus corrected.

"Whatever you call it, this is insane! I can't deal with this stuff when I have an audition tomorrow."

"Give me a day, and I will straighten this out," Eddie told her. "I'll make sure you won't get any assignments until things are back to normal."

Lena shook her head. "But what about Mrs. Katz? She's supposed to be dead!"

"The love boost must have given her soul a little more energy, but it is temporary. It'll all sort itself out."

"What if I hurt someone again like I did with that woman?" Marcus's voice wobbled. "I almost killed her."

"She will be fine," Eddie said, but he didn't sound very

convincing. "That should have never happened. Your power is designed to work only on the person it's intended for, and it can only be transferred when you are focused on your target. What happened today was a fluke."

"If it happened once, can't it happen again?" Lena asked.

"Kid, I will fix this," Eddie said flatly. "Give me a day." Then he hopped on his Segway and sped off, almost like he couldn't wait to get away.

chapter 8

"I can't believe he just left us here!" Lena said, staring after Eddie as he disappeared around a curve.

"Maybe we should kind of, um, stick together the next couple of days until this is all figured out." Now that Marcus was finally spending time with Lena again, he wasn't going to blow it. Even if it was under such crazy circumstances. Besides, how was he supposed to deal with all of this by himself?

Lena shook her head. "No way. I can't go around pretending to make people fall in love."

"What do you mean *pretending*?" Marcus asked. "What I do is as real as what you do."

"No offense," she said, tucking her hair behind her ears, "but death is a real, biological thing. Love is…well…"

Marcus's mouth sagged open. "Are you telling me you don't believe that love exists?"

"Our brains might think it does, but that's only chemicals tricking us into feeling things. It's not real. Trust me. My dad studies this stuff. He knows."

Marcus couldn't believe what he was hearing. "What about my grandparents? They were married for forty years, and they were the happiest people I knew." Grandma had died when Marcus was seven, so he didn't remember much about her, but he did have memories of his grandparents always smiling when they were together. And Grandpa still talked about Grandma Lily all the time. That had to be the real thing, right?

Lena shrugged. "Their brains were really good at making them think that."

"So what I do—what *all* matchmakers do—is a joke?" Marcus cried. He never thought he'd be yelling at the girl he had a crush on, but he couldn't stop himself.

Lena seemed to think his question through for a moment. "No," she finally said. "Obviously, you take it really seriously. It's…it's not for me, okay? So the sooner we figure out how to reverse this whole mix-up, the better."

She clearly didn't want to argue anymore, and Marcus didn't either. He was pretty sure Grandpa's book would strongly frown upon yelling at your date.

"I should go," Lena said, heading back toward the park entrance.

"Where are you going? Shouldn't we at least call the hospital and make sure Olivia is okay?" He reached into his pocket before remembering what had happened with Caspar. "Oh. I don't have my phone with me."

Lena stopped at a green bike that had been abandoned on the grass. She must have flung it aside before she'd rushed over to save Olivia from his glowing fingers.

"You're right. I guess we should check." Lena took out her phone, searched for the number to the hospital, and was talking to someone all in the span of a minute. Marcus marveled at her efficiency.

"I had to tell them I was her sister before they finally gave me info," Lena said, hanging up the phone a couple of minutes later. "She's still unconscious but stable."

Marcus sighed with relief. "So that means she's going to be okay?" If something really bad happened to that woman because of him…

"I think so. Maybe Eddie is right, and we don't have to worry." Lena picked up her bike and plopped her helmet on her head. "Okay, I need to go home and prep for my *Alice in Wonderland* audition tomorrow."

He couldn't believe she was worried about something so normal after everything that had happened. "But what about…? I mean, what are we supposed to *do*?"

Lena shook her head. "I have no idea, but I've spent weeks getting ready for this audition. I can't get distracted now."

How was she not still freaking out about everything that had happened? He definitely couldn't imagine going back to his house and acting like everything was fine. "I can walk you home if you want," he found himself saying, "and help you run lines."

Lena shrugged. "Sure. We're auditioning with the White Rabbit scene from the book. It starts with her saying, 'Mr. White Rabbit, where are you going?' And the rest of it goes like this." Then she launched into the monologue.

Marcus watched her mouth as she spoke the words. For some reason, the other parts of her face didn't move. She was saying the lines, but it didn't seem like she meant them.

"Well, what do you think?" she asked when it was over.

"Oh, um. Not bad."

She gave him a sharp look. "But not good either?"

"I didn't say that! Only...it seemed a little stiff, that's all."

"Stiff? What do you mean?"

Marcus knew he had to choose his words carefully. This was just like when his mom asked him for feedback on her trash sculptures and he had to try to find tactful ways of suggesting she make them look more like actual, recognizable things. "I don't know much about acting or anything, but maybe try putting some more feeling into it?"

Lena shrugged. "I don't want to overact. Directors hate that. But I'll try it again." She started from the beginning, saying the lines almost exactly the same way as before.

But Marcus wasn't listening anymore, because the enormity of what had happened hit him like a wrecking ball. He was a soul collector!

"So, how does it all work?" he asked, interrupting her.

Lena looked at him. "What do you mean?"

"If we're stuck with each other's powers for the next couple of days, shouldn't we know more about them? Like what does a soul collector actually *do*?"

She sighed. "I guess you're right. Well, what I do is pretty simple." Then she explained how she used the energy to "release" the soul from its body so that when the person died, his or her soul would go to the After.

"So you actually see the person's soul before you collect it?" he asked, thinking of the bright light bursting out of Ann-Marie that morning. Is that what he'd been seeing? Her soul?

"Just a flash of it. By the time I get there, the soul is so weak that it's barely glowing anyway," Lena said. "Eddie says it'll get easier to see my targets' souls once my powers get stronger."

Marcus nodded. That wasn't so different from his match-making auras. "What about car accidents and stuff? You're not saying soul collectors are in the car with those people, are you? I mean, they'd get hurt too."

"No, in accidental deaths like that, the soul is thrown out of the body. Then I'd get a message telling me to hurry over there to collect the soul before it wanders away."

"Wanders away?" he repeated. "Like…like the soul goes to haunt people?"

Lena shook her head. "It can get confused and drift around, that's all. If it gets too far away from the spot where it died and a soul collector can't find it, then soul hunters get involved."

"Like ghost hunters?"

"No, not ghosts," Lena insisted. "Ghosts are only in the movies. These are *souls* that aren't where they're supposed to be."

"You really don't like things you can't explain, do you?" Marcus asked. "Love. Ghosts. I bet you don't even believe that four-leaf clovers bring luck."

"They're genetic mutations," she said with a shrug. "How about you? What does a matchmaker do?"

He explained how the energy was a type of magnet that pulls two people together so they can get to know each other better. Then he told her how the first couple he'd ever matched had had a strong spark right away and how that spark had gotten even stronger the more time they had spent together, a sure sign that they were going to last.

When he was done, Lena let out a long sigh. "I guess that really is what happened to Mrs. Katz today. I'd been hoping whatever went wrong was something else, something that wouldn't mess up her life."

"Mess it up by making her fall in love instead of making her *die*?" Marcus asked in disbelief.

"I don't make people die. It's part of life. It happens."

"Well, so does love. Matchmakers only help it along. That's why we can't make people fall in love whenever we want." No matter how much Marcus had wished over the past few months that he could have "zapped" Lena with a little love jolt and made her like him, he knew it would do no good. The manual was clear that if you used the abilities for personal gain, they'd backfire.

"I'll have to check on Mrs. Katz later and make sure she's okay," said Lena.

"Why wouldn't she be okay? She's probably happier than she's ever been."

"Maybe she is now," said Lena, "but wait until the whole love cloud wears off. Then she'll be miserable."

Marcus couldn't believe how negative Lena was about this whole matchmaking thing. He'd always known she was matter-of-fact. That was one of the things he liked about her—along with her silky hair and her calm way of listening to people, even when they were shy like he was and never knew the right thing to say. When they'd worked on their math project together last spring, she'd been open to his ideas but had still kept them on track so they were done in no time. It was strange the things he was finding out about her now that they were together.

He sucked in a breath. Wait. *Were* they together? They'd kissed three times in the past twenty-four hours, after all. Granted, all three of those kisses had happened because of other people telling them what to do, but it still had to mean something, didn't it? Grandpa's book would certainly say they were "going steady."

He peered at Lena as she steered her bike down the street, mumbling lines from the play under her breath again. Maybe there was a reason behind all this power-swapping business. Maybe this was the universe's weird way of finally making Lena notice him.

"Why are you staring at me?" she asked suddenly, coming to a stop.

Marcus blinked. "Oh. Sorry. I guess I was…wondering why all this stuff is happening to us. What the bigger purpose is."

She raised an eyebrow. "You believe in that kind of thing? Fate and karma and all that?"

"I think sometimes things work out the way they're supposed to. Like when I make matches—"

Lena snorted. "That's someone else deciding what's supposed to happen. Eddie's boss picks two names out of a hat and tells you to pair them up. That's not exactly fate."

"Okay…well, what about when I see an old model spaceship at a flea market and it's missing a bunch of its parts. Why would I spend my allowance on it if I didn't think I could fix it?" he asked. Lena shook her head, clearly not understanding his point. "Because I know that even if I don't have the pieces I need now, I'll find them eventually. And then everything will work out."

Lena's eyes widened. "Wow. You're really an optimist, aren't you? No wonder they made you a cupid."

"Matchmaker," Marcus corrected. "No diaper, remember? I don't want my butt to look lumpy."

Finally, Lena cracked a smile. "How come you never made any jokes when we did our project together? You were always so quiet."

Marcus looked at the toes of his battered sneakers. "I guess I'm kind of shy when I don't know someone. But now that we're…I mean, you know something about me that no one else does."

"Yeah, I guess that's true," Lena said slowly. "I don't think anyone knows the real me anymore." She peered back at him, a hint of a smile still on her face, and he had the feeling that she really understood him. For the first time since Grandpa had gotten sick, the aching emptiness in Marcus's chest eased a little.

Suddenly, Lena's smile disappeared, like a door had shut somewhere inside her. "Come on. I have to get home," she said. Then she hurried her steps so that Marcus had to practically run to keep up.

chapter 9

On her doorstep, Lena turned to say good-bye to Marcus only to find him looking back at her with a weird expression on his face. He kept licking his lips and then glancing at the ground. Wait. Was he gearing up to kiss her again?

Not that she wanted him to. Or did she? No, of course not! The day had been too full of weirdness already. The best thing for Lena to do now was slip back into her house and hide.

"Well, I guess I'll see you at school tomorrow," she said.

"Oh...um, yeah." Marcus licked his lips again.

"Unless Eddie has news for us before then."

"Right." His amber eyes looked at her in a way that made her stomach feel oddly fluttery. Whatever was going on, she couldn't deal with it right now, not when her audition was just over twenty-four hours away.

"Bye!" she cried. Then she yanked open the door and practically slammed it in Marcus's face. She waited a second before peering through the peephole, letting out a whoosh of air when she saw him retreating down the driveway. For some reason, she was panting as she walked into the kitchen.

"Ah, Lena, there you are," her dad called from the living room. "What do you think of this outfit?"

She poked her head in to find him in the same kind of drab shirt and tie he wore to work every day. For a second, she had the crazy urge to tell her dad about everything that had happened. But of course, she couldn't. Even if she tried, he would never believe her.

"It looks okay," she said. "What's it for?"

"My lunch date, remember? I told you about it this morning?"

Had that really only been a few hours ago? How could Lena's entire life have changed between breakfast and lunch?

Her dad glanced at his watch and pushed his dark hair away from his forehead. "She should be here any minute."

"Wait, she's picking you up?" Her dad had never been all that traditional, but if he was letting the woman do all the work, then he really was indifferent to the whole idea of dating.

"We decided it was easiest that way."

"Well, have fun," Lena said.

"I will." But as he said the words, the world shifted again, and the air around her dad dulled and grayed. Lena stared at him as the awful feeling washed over her again, the sense of being hopelessly lonely.

"Dad?" she choked out. "Are you…are you okay?"

"Of course I am," he said in his usual reassuring tone, but she could suddenly hear how fake the words sounded. How had she never noticed it before?

When the gray cloud finally started to fade, Lena felt like the loneliness had seeped into her bones. Her whole body ached with it. What was going on? Did this have something to do with her new powers?

The doorbell rang, and her dad hurried to open the door. Meanwhile, Lena clung to the side of the couch, afraid that if she let go, she might fall over.

Dad's date swept into the hall like a gust of lavender-scented wind. She was tiny and decked out in a bright-red dress that perfectly contrasted with her jet-black hair. She definitely didn't look like a physicist.

Professor ran over to bring the woman a wad of used tissues, but she ignored him as she charged over to Lena.

"Hello! I'm Marguerite," she said as she enthusiastically shook Lena's hand.

"Um, hi," Lena said. Then she couldn't help adding stupidly, "Is your name French?"

"It is! My family is French Canadian, but I've lived in the States for years."

"Oh…" Lena realized she had nothing to say to that. She looked at her dad, who also seemed a little lost. This was the first time Lena had met any of her dad's dates, but she wondered if all of them were so perky.

"Shall we go?" Marguerite asked. "There's a lovely new place that opened up downtown. I think they have *crepes*." She pronounced the word in the French way that almost sounded like "craps." "And afterward, perhaps we can go see the new stamp exhibit at the museum?"

Lena stared. Not only was Marguerite a scientist like Dad, but she liked crepes and old stamps just like he did? Had Aunt Teresa coached Marguerite on what to say, or was she really this perfect?

Her dad nodded eagerly at Marguerite and smiled. That smile pierced through Lena like a laser. She realized it was the first real smile she'd seen on his face in months.

"Great!" Marguerite said. "Do you mind if I use your washroom before we go?" Then, without waiting for an answer, she disappeared down the hall.

"She seems nice," Lena whispered, the heavy feeling inside her finally fading.

Her dad's smile dimmed. "Don't worry. We won't be out too long."

"It's okay, Dad. Go have fun. I'll be fine," she found herself saying. Since when did she actually encourage her dad to go on dates? But this seemed different. *He* seemed different.

Or maybe all that mumbo jumbo Eddie and Marcus had spouted about love had seeped into her brain. Lena shuddered at the thought.

When Marguerite came out of the bathroom, her dad's face lit up all over again, and Lena found herself wishing he could look like that all the time instead of like the sad, serious person he'd become since Mom left.

"We'll be back in a bit," her dad said, showing Marguerite to the door.

"Have fun!" Lena said with a wave. And that's when it happened. Her fingers started to glow bright red just as her dad came over to give her his usual good-bye hug.

Oh no.

Before she could stop him, her dad wrapped his arms around her. The instant her hand brushed against him—*zap!*—the energy sank right into his body, as if it couldn't wait to burst out of her fingertips.

Her dad jumped back, like he'd gotten shocked by static electricity. Then he glanced at Marguerite, and the smile on his face bloomed into a grin.

When Marguerite looked back at him, Lena could actually

see the sparks flying between them, like tiny fireworks. Just like the ones between Mrs. Katz and the mailman.

Oh no. What had she done?

"Dad!" Lena cried. She had to take it back; she had to undo it. But how? She shook her fingers, willing them to light up again. Maybe if red zapped you with love juice, then another color—what was the opposite of red?—reversed it. But it was no use. She couldn't even make her fingers glow again.

"Don't worry, Chipmunk," her dad said, his voice sounding far away. "Everything will be all right." Then he took Marguerite's hand in his and disappeared through the door.

Lena stared after them for what felt like an hour. What had just happened? Had she zapped her own father with some kind of spell? But that was impossible! Eddie had said she wouldn't have any assignments, and Marcus had said you couldn't make people fall in love when they weren't meant to.

Fall in love.

The words bounced around in Lena's brain, clanging against the sides of her head. Love was fake. Love was chemicals. Love was a joke.

But then how could she explain what had happened before her eyes?

chapter 10

After dark, Marcus snuck over to Caspar's house and waded into the pond with a flashlight. He held his breath almost the whole time, convinced Caspar was going to come out of nowhere and corner him. But he had to take the risk. If his dad found out what had happened to the phone, Marcus would be grounded until high school.

After he'd succeeded in angering every frog in the pond, Marcus finally found his soggy phone. He shoved it into his pocket and sloshed all the way home. When he got there, he smuggled the phone into his room and put it into a plastic container. Then he dumped a box of Cajun rice on top and coughed at the cloud of spices that wafted into the air. He'd read that uncooked rice could pull the moisture out of electronics that had gotten wet. There wasn't any regular rice in the house, so the spicy Cajun stuff would have to do. He just hoped it worked. Otherwise, Eddie had no way to contact him except through Lena.

Lena. A warm feeling spread through Marcus's chest as he thought of having an excuse to talk to her again. He couldn't believe everything that happened today, but maybe this was finally his chance to "get the girl" as Grandpa Joe's book called it.

He tried to imagine what it would say in this situation. *Have you and the gal you like accidentally swapped powers? Try bringing her chocolates!*

He examined his fingers, looking for any hint of the strange purple glow that had been there before. Then he peered at himself in the full-length mirror on the back of his closet. He didn't look any different: same scrawny kid with messy hair and baggy jeans. No one would see him and think "soul collector." Then again, no one would have looked at him two days ago and thought "matchmaker." All they would have thought was "dork." If they'd thought anything at all.

He glanced at the empty terrarium on top of his dresser, and his chest tightened again.

What if Eddie was wrong? What if it wasn't so easy to switch back their powers? He couldn't take people's souls, no matter how natural Lena claimed it was. He couldn't even deal with a turtle dying without turning into a blubbering mess!

There was a knock on the door, making Marcus jump. He shoved the container of rice under his bed right before his dad poked his head in.

"Where'd you go off to after dinner?" his dad asked. "Your sister said you snuck out."

Figured Ann-Marie would tell on him.

"Oh, um." Marcus grabbed for any excuse he could think of. "I went for a run." It was sort of true. He had sprinted a good part of the way home, paranoid that Caspar would come after him.

His dad's eyebrows shot up. Then he leaned against the door frame, smugly crossing his arms in front of his chest. "So you finally decided to man up a little, huh?"

Marcus swallowed.

"How far'd you go?" his dad asked. The fact that his only son could barely run in a straight line had been a sore topic for years.

"N-not far," Marcus stammered. "Only, uh, a few miles. Three, maybe."

"Three?" His dad whistled. "Last time I tried to make you run, you couldn't even make it through one."

Oops. Well, that was it. His dad would call Marcus out on the lie and make him do push-ups as punishment, the whole time telling stories about how much worse his own father had punished him when he was young.

But surprisingly, Marcus's dad shrugged and said, "Maybe next year, we'll try you out for the track team." He thought for a second and added, "I'll have to time you beforehand though. The first year I tried out for hockey, I fell on my face in front of everyone, and my father said I'd embarrassed the whole family. We don't want history to repeat itself, do we?"

Marcus shook his head, stifling a sigh. The funny thing was, his dad actually thought he was going easy on Marcus. But since Mr. Torelli had been a high school hero back in his day—track star, hockey legend—he didn't seem to know what "going easy on someone" actually meant.

"Anyway," his dad went on, "your mother wanted me to tell you that we're going to the nursing home to see your grandfather tomorrow afternoon, so be ready after school."

"I can't. I have a lot of homework to do." At least this part was true.

"Homework can wait. Family can't," his dad said. "You're going." He turned to leave, but then his gaze fell on the moon ship on Marcus's worktable. "You still wasting your time on this nonsense?"

"It's not nonsense," Marcus said. "It's a hobby."

"A hobby is something useful, like collecting bottles and cans or getting a job. This…" He held up a lunar module that Marcus had finished painting last week and sighed. "This is a waste of time. What happened to doing Boy Scouts or joining the debate club? You never gave those things a chance."

Marcus swallowed. Over the years, he'd tried every sport and club his dad had come up with, and he'd failed miserably at every single one. He didn't want to think about the one—and only—Boy Scout camping trip he'd been on a few years ago when he'd gotten up to use the bathroom in the middle of the night and wound up lost in the woods until dawn. But his dad couldn't accept that his son was bad at those things. He thought Marcus only had to try harder.

"Grandpa built models when he was my age," Marcus said weakly.

His dad shook his head. "I know you and Joe get along, and that's fine. You should respect your elders, but that doesn't mean you need to be like them. Do you know what I'm saying?"

Marcus kept his lips tightly shut. Of course, his dad meant that he should grow up to be just like *him*. But the truth was, if Marcus could become half the man Grandpa Joe was, he'd be happy, no matter what his dad said.

"Did you go running in those old shoes?" his dad asked suddenly.

Marcus glanced over at the sneakers he'd worn every day since last year, still wet from this evening's trip to the pond. "Um, yeah."

"We can stop on the way home tomorrow and get you some proper running shoes."

"But—"

"If you're going to run, you're going to do it right," his dad said. Then he shut the door behind him.

Marcus sank down on his bed. Just when he'd finally fallen off his dad's sports radar, he'd put himself right back on it again.

If only his dad could know his secret, maybe he wouldn't be disappointed in him all the time. But as soon as he had the thought, Marcus realized how stupid it was. His dad would never be proud of a son who was a matchmaker. He'd think it was all "girlie hogwash."

And even now that Marcus literally had the power of life and death in his hands, it still wouldn't matter. To his family, he would always be a disappointment.

chapter 11

Lena couldn't wait to get to school in the morning. Her dad had spent all of breakfast singing show tunes and shuffling around the kitchen doing some kind of dance, all because of his date with Marguerite. He hadn't said much about it, but it had clearly gone well. The "zap" Lena had given him seemed to be going strong.

Ugh. She'd thought about sending Eddie a message and telling him what had happened, but he probably had his hands full trying to figure out how to undo their swapped powers. She didn't want to get him into bigger trouble. And if she was being honest, she didn't want to get herself into trouble either.

But maybe Marcus would be able to help. After all, he'd had this job a lot longer than she had.

As Lena waited in front of his locker, she spotted her friend Hayleigh lugging a sequined duffel bag down the hall. In truth, Hayleigh was more Abigail's friend than hers, but Lena liked her most of the time. As long as she didn't rope Lena into helping her with her crazy art projects.

"Hey, what are you doing?" Hayleigh asked. Not surprisingly, there was a streak of pink paint on her dark forehead. "Isn't your locker in the other hall?"

"I have to talk to Marcus for a minute."

Hayleigh gave her a knowing smile. "I still can't believe you guys kissed the other night!"

"Shh!" Lena said, glancing around. "The whole school doesn't need to know about it."

Hayleigh laughed. "Don't you think Connie Reynolds already told everyone?"

Lena covered her mouth, mortified at the thought of kids gossiping about her first kiss. The whole point of having her checklist was to avoid that kind of drama! Then again, if she hadn't started the stupid list, her dad wouldn't be cawing show tunes and flapping his arms and legs around the kitchen like a crazed bird.

Just then, she spotted Marcus rounding the corner. When he saw her, his whole face lit up. She couldn't help smiling back at him. She'd never met anyone else with such an infectious smile.

"Hey, Lena!" he said, a little too loudly. "How's it going? Your, um, your hair looks nice today."

"Oh, thanks," she said, touching her ponytail. Why was

Marcus always doing that? She couldn't let herself get distracted by compliments.

"Hey, Marcus!" Hayleigh chirped.

He jumped, as if he hadn't realized she was standing right there. "Oh, um, hi," he said, suddenly looking uncomfortable. "Wow, that bag is really shiny."

Hayleigh held it up proudly. "That's the point! Plus it fits all my art supplies. Do you like it?"

"Yeah…it's like a big mirror. But a bag. A mirror bag. I bet you could send messages into space with it." He chuckled softly, but Hayleigh only gave him a puzzled smile.

Lena couldn't stand the awkwardness for another second. "Marcus, I need to talk to you," she said.

"Well, I have to go bring this stuff to the art room," Hayleigh said, slinging the duffel bag back over her shoulder. "See you two later!" She gave them a little finger wave and then hurried away, giggling to herself.

Lena was relieved to see her disappear down the hall. "Come on," she told Marcus. "Let's go to the auditorium."

"Wait, I have something for you." He dug around in his backpack and pulled out a wilted rose, the end of its stem covered with aluminum foil. Then he held it out to her. "I wrapped the bottom in a paper towel, so if you rewet it later today, it should be fine until you bring it home."

Anna Staniszewski

Lena stared at the rose for a long moment. Even though its petals were crinkled, it was still beautiful. It was also the first flower any guy had ever given her. "Wow, th-thank you," she said, carefully taking it in her fingers. Her chest seemed to tingle with sudden warmth, and for some reason, she had the weird urge to hug the flower like some giddy girl in a movie might do.

"Sorry it's kind of in rough shape," Marcus said. "It was the craziest thing, but I think I accidentally killed the whole bush when I touched it."

Lena's eyes snapped up, the warm feeling in her chest vanishing.

"What do you mean you killed the rosebush by touch-ing it?"

He shrugged. "It must be your powers. Or, um, *my* powers now, I guess. My fingers started glowing for no reason, and then the entire plant wilted right in front of me."

"But that's crazy! You shouldn't be able to do stuff like that." Lena sucked in a breath. Then again, she shouldn't have been able to make her dad randomly fall in love with someone, but it had happened. "I think things are even more messed up than we realized. Come on." She waved Marcus toward the auditorium, which was always empty this time of day.

"What's wrong?" he asked when they were perched in the back row.

Lena slumped in her musty seat and told him all about what had happened with her dad the day before.

"Whoa," he said when she was done. "So you gave him a love boost?"

"Don't call it that. It sounds so cheesy!"

"Call it what you want, this is serious. There's no way to undo it."

"Are you sure? What about the manual Eddie gave you? There has to be something in it."

Marcus shook his head. "The only thing you can do now is wait for the spark between them to fade on its own. If they're not an actual love match, it shouldn't take long." He gave her an examining look. "But this woman sounds kind of perfect for your dad. Is it really so bad if he's happy?"

"He's not happy! He only thinks he is. He was fine before I did this to him." Even as she said the words, Lena wasn't sure they were true. After all, she'd felt all that loneliness coming from her dad yesterday. But his whole personality had changed since she'd zapped him. That had to mean this love stuff was a scam, right? Some kind of hypnosis? Once she had her regular dad back, then she could find a way to make him less lonely. Maybe they could get another dog or something.

"Have you heard from Eddie?" Marcus asked.

Lena shook her head. "Nothing yet. You?"

"Um, my phone's out of commission right now."

"We should let him know what's going on. Our powers are obviously out of control. And just in case, we should avoid touching other people."

"Even each other?" Marcus asked.

"Probably, just to be on the safe side." The homeroom bell rang, making Lena jump. "Oh no! I was supposed to meet Abigail to practice for auditions!"

"Right, that's today. What do theater people say? 'Break a leg' or something?"

"You can wish me luck. All that superstition stuff is—"

"I know! I know!" Marcus said, and for some reason, he was smiling. "You don't believe in love, ghosts, or superstitions."

"What, are you keeping a list?" Lena asked.

Marcus's smile grew wider. "Maybe. How else am I going to unravel the mysteries of Lena Perris?"

She couldn't help smiling back. "I'm pretty sure that besides the whole secret identity thing, I'm the least mysterious person at this school."

"That's exactly what you want people to think," he said. "It probably means you collect human skulls in your basement. Or worse, stuffed unicorns."

Lena laughed. Ever since Connie Reynolds had shoved them into that closet, Marcus had seemed different, more sure of himself. She wished other people could see this side of him. Then maybe her friends wouldn't call him a weirdo anymore.

"Wait, I know!" Lena cried, something clicking in her brain. "We need to get Connie Reynolds involved."

"With your audition?" Marcus asked, his brow crinkling.

"No! She was there the first time we kissed. Maybe she needs to be there again, so that our powers switch back."

Marcus seemed to think this over. "But does that mean we have to re-create the whole party too? Maybe it all has to be exactly the same as the first time. That's pretty much impossible."

He was right. "I'll keep thinking about it," Lena said, getting to her feet. "Oh, and Marcus. Um, thanks again for the flower. That was really nice of you." Then she rushed out of the auditorium without looking back.

Even though she was already late, Lena stopped at her locker and carefully tucked Marcus's rose inside. She didn't want it to get more crushed in her bag. For some reason, she had the urge to wave good-bye to it before she shut the locker door, like it might be sad all alone in the dark. But she told herself to stop being ridiculous. She couldn't be one of those girls who got all mushy the minute a guy did something nice for them. *I'm not going to be weak like that*, she told herself as she slammed the locker door shut and hurried down the hallway.

When Lena got to homeroom, Mrs. Lo looked up from her

desk and gave a disapproving shake of her head before marking something down in her book. Lena blushed as she slunk to her seat. She'd never been late for anything in her life. Her dad liked to remind her that she'd even been born early.

"Where were you?" Abigail asked over the dull roar of the other kids laughing and talking around them. "I waited at your locker."

"Sorry, I had to, um, talk to someone. Oh! I forgot!" Lena fished around in her bag and took out the quilted purse she'd made for Abigail the night before. She was careful not to brush Abigail's hand when she handed it over. If her fingers could flare up at any second, she had to be extra cautious. The last thing she needed was Abigail going gaga over some guy.

"Wow, thanks. What's this for?" Abigail asked.

"It's a thank-you for dragging me to Connie's party. Otherwise, I would have never gotten my first kiss." Granted, if she hadn't gone to that party, none of the other stuff would have happened, but that wasn't Abigail's fault.

Should she tell Abigail what was going on? Eddie had made her swear not to reveal her soul collector identity to anyone, not even her best friend, but this situation was so insane. It would be a relief to tell someone.

"You know, Marcus is kind of cute," Abigail said. "Even if he is pretty awkward. I could see why you like him."

"I don't like him," Lena insisted.

"Well, Hayleigh and I were talking last night, and if you're not interested in him…do you think he might like one of us?"

Lena gawked at her. "What are you talking about?" Is that why Hayleigh had been so friendly to Marcus in the hall?

Abigail shrugged. "I mean, if he's your property, that's fine. We'll back off."

"I…" For some reason, Lena couldn't form words. Why should she care if her friends liked Marcus? Sure, only two days ago, they'd been laughing at her for kissing him, but what did it matter to her if they were suddenly interested in him? Her friends could do whatever they wanted.

But when she tried to tell Abigail that, the words still wouldn't come out.

"Okay, never mind," Abigail finally said, probably getting tired of watching Lena gulping air like a fish. "Obviously you like him."

"I don't like him!" Lena cried. Everyone in the room turned to look at her. Lena felt her cheeks go bright red, but she ignored the other kids' stares and said in a loud voice, "Are we running lines or not?"

Abigail shrugged and fished out a copy of the monologue. "People have crushes on other people, you know. It's totally normal."

Lena didn't answer. Instead, she pretended to read over the audition scene. So much for telling Abigail about what was happening with her. Her friend clearly wouldn't understand. It seemed that when it came to this whole supernatural mess, the only person on Lena's team was Marcus.

chapter 12

By the time the bell for last period rang, Lena had her nerves under control. She'd gone over the Alice monologue in the bathroom between classes, she'd spent all of lunch in the auditorium practicing, and she'd made sure to stay nice and hydrated throughout the day so that her throat wouldn't be dry and raspy.

She was ready. As she waited in the auditorium for the auditions to start, she couldn't help imagining what things would be like once she got into the play. Her dad would be so proud of her that maybe he'd finally stop being the Tin Man for a minute and show some real emotion (without the help of any fake love spells). And her mom might even come see her on opening night instead of just doing her once-a-year visit on Christmas. But most of all, Lena would know that her dream of becoming a real actress one day wasn't just some crazy fantasy. It could really come true.

When everyone was gathered in the auditorium, Mr. Jackson stood up on the stage, holding a clipboard and adjusting his red bow tie.

"All right!" he called out. "Put your names on this sign-up sheet, and I'll call you one by one."

There was a frantic dash to the clipboard as Mr. Jackson put it on top of the piano. Lena made sure to stand back so she wouldn't accidentally brush against anyone, which meant that by the time she got to the sign-up sheet, she was the only one left. She scrawled her name after Abigail's and went to sit in the front row.

Then the waiting began. Abigail spent the whole time reading the monologue over and over, but Lena watched every audition, trying to decide who Mr. Jackson would cast for all the parts. She had a feeling that Emery Higgins would be the Cheshire Cat because of the gleaming braces on his enormous smile.

With each girl who auditioned for Alice, Lena's confidence grew. None of them were that great. The girl who'd gotten the lead last year was now in high school, which meant that Lena might actually have a shot. But getting the lead wasn't the point, she reminded herself. Any part in the play would do. That's all she wanted.

Finally, almost two hours later, it was Abigail's turn. The auditorium was pretty empty, since most kids had left after they'd auditioned.

"Break a leg," Lena whispered as her friend headed up to the stage. She'd given Marcus a hard time about using that phrase, but she knew Abigail would be offended if she wished her good luck.

Abigail stood in the center of the stage with her eyes closed for a minute, like she was meditating. Then she took a deep breath and started to speak, not as herself, but as Alice.

Lena watched her, mesmerized, along with everyone else in the auditorium. Abigail was amazing. She even looked the part with her long, blond hair and bright-blue eyes. This was a far cry from the self-conscious girl who'd practically whispered her lines at last year's audition.

"Wow!" Mr. Jackson said when she was finished. "You've come a long way!"

"Thanks," Abigail said with a shy glance up from the stage. "I've been practicing a lot."

Mr. Jackson scribbled something on his clipboard and then called out, "Finally, Lena Perris!"

Lena got to her feet and passed by Abigail, who seemed to be floating to her seat. Her friend didn't even look at her, as if she were still lost in Wonderland.

Don't think about her, Lena told herself. *Focus on your own audition.*

When she got to the center of the stage, her heart started

bouncing off the sides of her chest like a basketball. She hadn't felt nervous before, but now she could barely breathe.

She glanced out at the crowd, and suddenly she noticed the colors shifting around her. *Oh no. Please, don't let this happen now.*

But it was too late. Suddenly, two eighth graders in the back of the auditorium were glowing yellow, sparks fluttering between them. Had Marcus zapped them recently? And a sixth-grade girl in the middle row had a pale gray aura around her as she stared at a skinny seventh grader with an odd, hungry look on her face.

Lena closed her eyes. *Stop it.*

"Is everything all right?" Mr. Jackson called.

Lena forced her eyes open and sighed in relief when she saw the auras were gone. "Fine," she said. "Sorry. I'm ready."

Then she cleared her throat and pushed Alice's words out of her mouth. They oozed out slowly at first, like molasses, but then they began to pour out more quickly until finally she wasn't thinking about them anymore, she was just saying them. Before she knew it, the monologue was over.

She expected Mr. Jackson to tell her "good job" or at least to say "thank you" like he had to all the other kids, but he only glanced at the sign-up sheet and said, "Looks like that's it for today. I'll have the cast list posted tomorrow morning."

As Lena staggered to her seat, she spotted Eddie in the back of the auditorium, waving to her. Then he ducked out into the hall. Why was he here?

She quickly told Abigail "good job" and then rushed outside. She found Eddie examining the trophy case near the main office.

"Do you think one day they will give trophies for hoverboarding?" he asked dreamily. "Imagine a whole team of kids flying around a track."

"What are you doing here?" Lena asked.

Eddie turned to her, his face growing serious. "The boss lady called me. She said the situation has gotten worse?"

Lena nodded. "Our powers are acting up for no reason. I mean, Marcus killed a rosebush just by touching it!"

Eddie gave her a skeptical look. "Things like that should not happen. It's not possible."

"But they *are* happening. I kept seeing auras during my *Alice* audition, and you don't even want to know what's going on with my dad."

"It has to be from you two getting your wires crossed." Eddie shook his head. "This is serious. If your powers are flaring up when they are not supposed to, that could throw off the whole balance of things."

"You mean we're going to cause a black hole or something?"

"Not exactly, but there is an order to how things are supposed to happen. The more you change that order, the harder it is to make everything right again. Next time you feel your powers acting up, the two of you need to control them, okay? Take deep breaths and focus on calming the energy."

"That's it? We could accidentally make the world explode, and you're saying we need to take deep breaths?"

Eddie gave her a look that was so helpless, Lena suddenly felt bad. Her boss seemed as lost in the whole situation as she was.

"You said you were on probation before," she said softly. "Was it for something like this?" It was probably none of her business, but if this had happened before, she wanted to know how long it would take to get everything back to normal.

Eddie shook his head. "I was helping out an old friend, but unfortunately, the boss lady did not see it that way. She was finally starting to forget about all of that when this mess happened."

"Marcus and I had an idea," Lena said, "but I don't know if it's even possible." Then she told him about re-creating Connie Reynolds's party.

When she was done, Eddie absently clicked his tongue, deep in thought. "I will see what I can do," he said finally. "In the meantime, be careful."

As he turned to go, Lena couldn't help calling after him. "Hey, Eddie. You saw my audition, right? How did I do?"

"You were good, kid," Eddie called over his shoulder, flashing her a smile. But as he disappeared around the corner, she couldn't help thinking that he hadn't sounded all that convincing.

chapter 13

The nursing home was even worse than Marcus had feared. It was a maze of nondescript hallways and people in uniforms bustling by, pushing ancient-looking folks in wheelchairs. It felt like there was no air in the whole building, like he'd walked into a crypt or something.

As Marcus and his family headed to Grandpa Joe's room, his mom chattered on about some new papier-mâché technique she wanted to try out. Meanwhile, his sister shot him a dirty look and said, "I was hoping to bring Grandpa some of my red roses, but *someone* poisoned them."

"I didn't!" Marcus protested, but he knew it was no use. How could he convince Ann-Marie that he hadn't hurt her prized rosebush when he *had* been the one to kill it? She wouldn't care that it had been an accident.

Finally, when Marcus thought he might pass out from the lack of oxygen in the air, his family stopped at a dimly lit room at the end of a long corridor.

"Pop?" Marcus's mom said as they went in. "Are you awake?"

Grandpa Joe turned to them from his bed, his watery eyes lighting up. "Look who's here!" he said.

The rest of his family went into the room, but Marcus stood frozen in the doorway. This couldn't be Grandpa Joe. He was so small in that enormous bed that he looked like a frail old man. A stranger.

"Marcus, my boy," Grandpa said. "Get on in here so I can see you." At least his voice sounded the same.

Marcus forced his legs to start moving again. He forced his eyes to stay on Grandpa instead of focusing on the floor. He forced himself to smile a little.

"Hi," he whispered.

"I was hoping you'd come by soon," Grandpa said. "The entertainment here hasn't been up to snuff."

"Hey!" Ann-Marie said. "What about all those jokes I told you the other day?"

Grandpa laughed. "Your sister's got quite the repertoire of puns, Marcus. Did you know that?"

"She probably memorized a joke book so she could be the best at that too," he found himself grumbling.

His dad gave him a sharp look, and Marcus stopped talking for the rest of the visit.

Grandpa soon launched into a story about flirting with one of the staff members until she agreed to give him two cups of pudding instead of only one. The rest of the family laughed, and if Marcus had been hearing this story anywhere else, he would have been laughing the loudest. But all he could do now was keep a vague smile on his face and avoid actually looking at Grandpa.

How could his parents and sister laugh as if everything were normal? The only time Marcus had even cracked a smile these past few weeks had been with Lena, and that felt wrong now that he was here.

Finally, after what seemed like hours, it was time to go.

"Hang back a minute, would you, Marcus?" Grandpa asked.

The rest of the family filed out into the hallway, leaving Marcus all alone with Grandpa in a room that suddenly felt too small and too hot.

"You all right, son?" Grandpa asked.

"I'm fine," he mumbled. "Are *you* okay?"

Grandpa let out a dry laugh. "Oh, you know. I've been better. But I'm glad you came. How are the models coming along?"

Marcus swallowed. "I'm still working on the moon ship," he said. "I haven't had a lot of time since…" He trailed off. As much as he wanted to, he couldn't tell Grandpa what had been going on the past few days. "I'm sorry I haven't come to see you. I wanted to, really, but I..."

Grandpa's eyes sparkled a little as if he understood why Marcus had been staying away. "How are things working out with the girl you told me about? What's her name? Elaine?"

"Lena," Marcus said, an embarrassed smile pulling at his lips despite himself. "Um, things are good, I guess. We're hanging out a lot more. She's kind of hard to read though. Just when I think she might like me, something happens and then I'm not sure again."

"Well, you stick with that book I gave you, and it'll all work out," Grandpa said, his voice growing drowsy. "You'll see." Then he reached out his hand, and—before Marcus could pull away—rested it on top of his.

Marcus was too paralyzed to move, but luckily his fingers stayed normal and unglowing. After a minute, he even managed to give Grandpa's hand a reassuring squeeze in return.

Soon, Grandpa's eyes drifted closed, and his soft snores filled the room.

When Marcus finally forced himself to look—really look—at Grandpa Joe, the air around the old man seemed to darken. And Marcus could actually *see* it, his grandpa's soul, barely clinging to his sleeping body, getting ready to be collected so it could move on.

Marcus slid his hand out of Grandpa's and ran for the door.

"What's wrong?" he heard his mom call, but he didn't stop. He kept running and running until he reached the end of the hallway and couldn't go any farther. Then he collapsed into a chair and started to cry.

His mom had been trying to convince Marcus that Grandpa would be okay, but he knew what he'd seen. That faint pinprick of a soul, so different from Ann-Marie's, meant Grandpa's time was almost up. And there was nothing Marcus could do about it.

chapter 14

Lena peered at the cast list from down the hall. Other kids kept clustering around to check it, not giving her an opportunity to read it when no one else was there. She'd even gotten to school early so she'd have a better chance of being alone.

Finally, the hallway cleared, and she dashed in front of the list. At the top, in big, mocking letters, was Abigail's name. She'd been cast as Alice.

Lena's heart sagged. *Don't be stupid*, she told herself. Of course Abigail had been cast in the lead; she was perfect for it. Lena scanned the entire list, but her name wasn't there. She scanned it again, slower this time, but it still wasn't there. How was this possible? She'd worked so hard!

It had to be a mistake. That was the only explanation.

She turned on her heel and marched down the hall to Mr. Jackson's classroom. She found him in the corner of the room, sorting through stacks of dusty books that looked like moths had been nesting in them.

"Lena, what can I do for you?" he asked.

"I think there was a mistake with the casting."

Mr. Jackson furrowed his brow. "A mistake?"

"I wasn't on the list."

"Oh." He sighed and put down a tattered copy of *Romeo and Juliet*. "Lena, I appreciate how hard you've been trying. I really do. And I wish I'd had a part for you this year, but the cast is so small that it simply wasn't possible."

Lena squeezed the checklist in her pocket, the one with "make the school play" written right at the top. "So I really didn't get in?" she whispered.

"Not this time. I'm sorry. But the high school productions are much bigger. You should try next year."

"What did I do wrong?" she asked.

Mr. Jackson let out a soft chuckle and adjusted his bow tie—blue today. "You didn't do anything wrong."

"That's obviously not true. If I'd been good enough, I would have gotten in. I want to know what I can do better. That's what scientists do. They figure out why something failed so they can improve on it next time."

"Lena…" She didn't like the way he kept saying her name, like he was trying to protect her from the truth.

"Please tell me!" she said. "I can handle it."

"You've always been a little stiff, that's all," Mr. Jackson said finally. "If you work on putting more emotion into your acting, really let loose, I think it will open up a lot of opportunities for you."

"Stiff?" She cringed, remembering how Marcus had said the same thing. But it couldn't be true. She'd put everything she had into her monologue. It was her stupid new matchmaking power's fault. If she hadn't been so distracted by everyone's auras, she would have been able to concentrate on her audition.

"I was having a hard time focusing yesterday. Can't you give me another chance?"

"I'm sorry, Lena. I wish I could, but it wouldn't be fair to everyone else. I'm sure you'll get in next time." It was exactly what he'd said to her last year. The bell rang, and Mr. Jackson got to his feet. "Time to get to homeroom, okay?" There was a pleading tone in his voice, like he was begging her to let it go.

"Fine." As she marched down the hallway, her head started throbbing. This was all because of the mess with Marcus. Why had she ever kissed him? Now everything was ruined.

Just then, she spotted Abigail walking away from the cast list. No, she wasn't walking. She was *prancing*.

"Lena!" Abigail cried when she saw her. "I got it! I got the lead!"

"I saw. Congratulations," Lena said, trying to smile.

"This is perfect! Hayleigh's doing costumes, so we'll all get to hang out!" Her face was shining like a beacon. Lena wanted to be happy for her—she *was* happy for her—but she couldn't help the gnawing feeling inside her.

"Wait," Abigail added, as if finally realizing that something was wrong. "You got in too, didn't you? I didn't actually check the whole list."

Lena shook her head. "Next year," she said weakly.

"Oh! Right. Next year, you'll get in for sure! You can do props again this time. That'll be fun, right?"

As they headed down the eighth-grade hallway, they passed Brent Adamson standing at his locker. His plump lips were on display as he chewed a piece of gum, which was totally not allowed in school. When he spotted Abigail, he gave her a thumbs-up. "Congrats on the play," he said.

Abigail waved at him and giggled—actually giggled!

The gnawing feeling inside Lena's chest turned to chomping anger. Not only was Abigail in the play, but now Brent Adamson was suddenly paying attention to her?

It was all too much. Lena wanted time to rewind to last week, before she'd ever kissed Marcus Torelli, even if it did mean having to uncheck "first kiss" on her list. She should have waited for Brent Adamson instead. Then everything would have gone according to plan.

Or maybe…

Maybe she couldn't turn back time, but she could check things off her list the right way. So far, her new powers had only made her life worse. Maybe she could use them to make things a little better.

She stopped in the middle of the hallway and smiled when she spotted Brent Adamson coming toward her. His friends were nowhere in sight.

"Lena, what are you doing?" Abigail asked.

"Um, nothing. You go ahead, okay? I'll catch up."

Abigail looked uncertain, but then the bell rang again, and she hurried away.

As Brent got closer, Lena put her hand behind her back and willed the energy into her fingertips. They instantly flared with prickly heat, like they'd been waiting for her to use her new power again. Luckily, most kids were in homeroom already, so she didn't have to worry about anyone seeing.

"Hey, Brent!" she said, getting into position. Somewhere in the back of her mind echoed Eddie's warnings about the balance of the universe, but she pushed them down. Things were already royally messed up. Why couldn't she at least get something good out of this whole disaster?

When Brent turned toward her, Lena reached out and gently touched his arm. Instantly, she could feel the energy drain out of her and into him.

Brent stopped as if he'd been struck by lightning. He didn't move, only stared at her like a statue.

"Brent?" She stepped in front of him so that her eyes were directly in line with his. "Are you okay?"

She expected him to react the way the mailman had when he'd looked at Mrs. Katz. She expected him to get a glazed-over look on his face. She even sort of expected him to have cartoon hearts coming out of his chest.

But none of those things happened.

Instead, Brent Adamson backed away from her with a sudden look of green-tinged horror on his face. And then he fled.

chapter 15

Marcus couldn't believe he was late for homeroom again thanks to Caspar Brown. The oaf had grabbed Marcus's backpack in the school parking lot and thrown it into a Dumpster. Then he'd hooted with laughter and told Marcus to go find it.

Now, smelling worse than one of his mom's art projects, Marcus hurried down the hall, hoping Miss Ryan wouldn't mark him late. The last thing he needed right now was detention.

Then he saw something that made him forget all about getting in trouble: Lena in the middle of the hallway next to Brent Adamson, her fingers glowing bright red. As Marcus stared in shock, she reached out and zapped Brent with a love bolt.

An instant later, Brent staggered back and took off running down the hallway, right past where Marcus was still standing.

"Dude," Brent said as he darted by, holding his stomach.

"You stink." Then he veered into the boys' bathroom, and the door slammed shut behind him.

Lena came rushing after him. "Marcus, get out of the way," she said. "Something's wrong! I zapped Brent, and he ran off!"

But Marcus didn't move. "Did you zap him so that he'd be into you?"

Lena's cheeks grew noticeably pink. "Yeah, so? What's the point of having these powers if I can't use them to my advantage?"

"Because they don't work that way! If you use your powers for personal gain, they backfire."

She looked at him. "Backfire? What do you mean?"

"The manual says that the powers have the opposite effect if you use them for your own benefit."

"But that doesn't make sense! I used them on my dad yesterday, and they worked fine."

"That's because you were doing it for your dad, not for you." Marcus let out a sputtering sigh. "I can't believe you've had my powers for a day, and you've already zapped two people you weren't supposed to!"

She looked down at the floor, and he instantly felt bad. He hadn't meant to snap at her, but this was all too much. Here he thought things were finally going well between them and now she was trying to make other guys fall in love with her?

"It was an accident," she said softly. "At least, the first one was. This thing with Brent… I don't know what that was."

"I thought you didn't believe in all this love stuff anyway."

"I don't!" Lena said. She closed her eyes and took in a long breath. "I guess I was trying to make my horrible day a little better."

"Why, what happened?" Then he remembered. "The play."

She nodded. "I didn't get in."

"I'm sorry," he said, and he was. He could tell how important the play was to her. "But how is zapping Brent going to fix anything?"

"It was supposed to help me with my list."

"What list?"

Lena shook her head. "Forget it. It's nothing." She sniffed the air. "Why do you smell like rotten fruit?"

But he wasn't going to let her change the subject. "What list?"

Lena reluctantly pulled a piece of paper out of her pocket. "This one." She handed it to him, and his breath caught in his chest as he scanned the lines of neat handwriting.

"First kiss? First dance? First date? What is this?" he whispered.

"Milestones," she said. "All the coming-of-age stuff I wanted to do this year."

He blushed as he noticed that "first kiss" had been checked

off with his name written in red beside it. But then he realized what this meant. "What was Brent going to be?"

"First date, maybe?" she said, shrugging. "I didn't totally think it through. And obviously, it was a mistake." She glanced at the door to the boys' bathroom, but Brent still hadn't come out. "Do you think he's okay in there?"

Marcus folded the list carefully and handed it back to Lena, trying not to let her see how crushed he was. Of course, the kiss had just been something she'd wanted to check off her list. For all he knew, she'd had her eye on Brent Adamson all along. How stupid he'd been yesterday, telling Grandpa Joe that he thought Lena might actually like him.

"Marcus?" she asked. "Are you okay? Your face is kind of blueish."

So much for playing it cool. What would Grandpa's book say about the situation? Something about not being a sore loser, probably. Accepting defeat gracefully. He wasn't sure what else to do.

He let out a long breath. "I'll go check on Brent."

"Are…are you sure?" Lena asked, suddenly looking puzzled.

"Yeah. But I told you, whatever you did to him probably didn't work." He spun around and went into the bathroom.

At first it was silent, and Marcus wondered if Brent had jumped out the window. According to the manual, backfires could be pretty extreme, so he wouldn't be surprised. But then he heard a toilet flush, and Brent came out, wiping his mouth. His face was red, and his eyes were watery.

"Hey, are you okay?" Marcus asked.

"Yeah," Brent said, his voice hoarse. "I totally puked for no reason."

"Oh…sorry." This was who Lena had wanted to fall in love with her? Some guy who sounded like he'd just stumbled off a surfboard?

"I guess I should stop eating tacos for breakfast." Brent chuckled before splashing water on his face.

Marcus returned a weak smile before ducking back out of the bathroom. Lena was still waiting in the hallway with an anxious look on her face.

"Well?" she asked. "Is he okay? Did I kill him?"

Marcus shook his head. "I think he got sick, that's all. Maybe it had nothing to do with you."

But at that moment, the bathroom door swung open and Brent appeared. He took one look at Lena, and the color drained out of his face. "Oh no," he said, covering his mouth. Then he turned and hurried back into the bathroom.

chapter 16

Pedaling home from school, Lena still couldn't believe what had happened. Brent Adamson was supposed to think he was in love with her, not get sick at the sight of her! And now, according to Marcus, all she could do was wait until her zap faded.

As if that wasn't bad enough, Marcus had been weirdly quiet around her ever since he'd found out about the Brent thing. Was it possible he was jealous of her wanting Brent to like her? Is that why she'd felt so guilty when Marcus had figured out what she'd done?

No, that was crazy. Like she'd told Abigail, she and Marcus were friends. Friends didn't get jealous or feel guilty about spending time with other people. The last thing Lena needed was more love nonsense like that in her life. She had plenty as it was with the Mrs. Katz situation.

As Lena stopped by the old woman's house to check on

her, not surprisingly she spotted a mail truck parked in the driveway. Lena peeked in through the window and gasped. Mrs. Katz and the mailman were ballroom dancing around the living room. It was midafternoon, but they were all decked out in formal wear.

How could people let love do this to them? It was disgusting!

With a sigh, Lena got on her bike and headed home. When she walked in the door, she wasn't expecting to see her dad back from work, and she definitely wasn't expecting him to be packing a picnic basket. She didn't even know they *owned* a picnic basket.

"What are you doing here?" she asked as Professor ran over to deliver a chewed-up sneaker at her feet. It looked suspiciously like the one that had mysteriously disappeared from her closet a year ago. Then, as usual, he went back to his squirrel lookout in front of the sliding glass door.

"I'm playing hooky this afternoon," her dad said. "Marguerite's on her way over. We're going to have a late lunch in the park."

Lena couldn't remember the last time her dad had taken any time off from work except when she was sick. This had to be the matchmaking hypnosis in action. "So you like her?"

Her dad grinned. "I suppose I do."

"What do you like about her?" Lena asked, suddenly curious

about how all this matchmaking stuff actually worked. Did it completely blind you to the other person's faults, or did it make you like everything about him or her, no matter what it was?

"Well…" Her dad thought about it for a minute. "I suppose it's nice to have a fellow scientist to talk to. Plus, Marguerite was married before, so we have that in common. And we like the same classic British science fiction shows—I've never met anyone else who liked those. But mostly…I guess I enjoy the companionship."

"Is it the same way it was with Mom?" Lena asked.

She expected her dad's smile to fade like it always did when she brought up her mother, but he only said, "I suppose in some ways it is, although Marguerite is a much more upbeat person. She's easier to be around."

Lena nodded, remembering how sad her mom had been so much of the time. Even doing simple things like going to the grocery store had seemed to bring her down. Lena would constantly try to cheer her mom up, but it clearly hadn't done any good in the end.

"Wait, what are you doing home?" her dad asked, glancing at the time. "I thought you'd have play practice."

She shook her head. "No luck this time."

"I'm sorry, Chipmunk."

She blinked at him. This was the second time he'd used

the nickname in two days. "You haven't called me Chipmunk in years."

"I haven't?" He laughed. "Well, I suppose you're not as tiny as you were when I first gave you that name. And you don't hoard nearly as much food."

"I think you made that part up anyway. There's no way I could have snuck all those peanuts into my crib."

Her dad gave her a sympathetic smile. "I'm sorry you didn't get into the play, Chipmunk. You know I love you no matter what, don't you?"

Lena stared. Her dad never used the L-word, not in a non-scientific way anyway.

"I thought you said love is only chemicals."

He ran his hand over his bald spot. "The love that parents have for their children isn't simply chemical; it's biological. It's a matter of survival of the species. There's nothing more important."

"So do you think you could love Marguerite? Even after everything with Mom?"

Finally, her dad's smile dimmed. He seemed confused all of a sudden. "I...I don't know. Part of me thinks I couldn't, but there's another part of me...that thinks maybe I could."

Lena could practically see her matchmaking voodoo working against her dad's normal thoughts. She suddenly felt terrible that she'd messed with his emotions like that.

"Dad, can you do me a favor and not hang out with Marguerite for a few days?" Once the "love boost" wore off, then he could go on all the dates he wanted. At least Lena would know that what he was feeling was real and not something she'd caused by accident.

Her dad frowned. "But I already made plans with her for today. She'll be here any second."

"Tell her you're sick or something."

Her dad's eyebrows went up. "What is this all about? I thought you said you wanted me to spend time with her."

"I...I don't want you to rush into things." Besides, if she found her dad and Marguerite ballroom dancing in the house, she'd scream.

"No one is rushing," her dad said. "We're just having a picnic."

"Please, Dad." She felt tears stinging at her eyes before she quickly blinked them away. Lena couldn't remember the last time she'd cried, and she wasn't about to do it now.

Clearly, Dad was surprised to see her so emotional too. "What's going on, Chipmunk? Is this about the play?"

"Yeah, I guess, and about other stuff." She wished, yet again, that she could tell him what was going on. Of course, his scientist brain could never accept all the crazy supernatural things she'd been dealing with. But in a way, it would be a relief to have him tell her that none of it was real. Maybe then she could fool herself into believing that for a little while.

But even if she had gotten up the courage to tell him the truth, the doorbell rang, and it was too late. Marguerite waltzed in wearing a checkered sundress, exactly the kind of thing you'd expect someone to wear to a picnic.

"Are we ready to go?" she cooed at Lena's dad, ignoring Professor, who was trying to regift his old sneaker offering.

Her dad gave Lena a questioning look. She could tell he wanted to go—voodoo or no voodoo—but that he wouldn't if she asked him not to. But the hopeful look on his face shut her up. Yes, maybe all this love business was fake, but her dad seemed happy. She was sure that if she checked out his aura, it would be a hundred times lighter than it had been the other day. She couldn't take that away from him, could she?

"Have fun, Dad," she told him. "I'll be fine."

"Are you sure?"

Lena nodded, and he gave her a warm smile. She couldn't remember the last time her dad had looked at her like that. She hadn't realized how much she'd missed it.

As she watched Dad and Marguerite leave for their date, Professor came over and rubbed up against Lena's leg. She absentmindedly scratched behind his ears, marveling at everything that had happened the past few days. The whole power-swapping fiasco had messed things up with Brent Adamson and ruined her chances of getting into the play, but if her dad was finally happy, then maybe it wasn't all bad after all.

chapter 17

Marcus walked home from school the longest way he could think of. If he took his time, maybe he'd avoid seeing Caspar Brown. He was starting to wonder if Caspar had put a tracking device on him or something. How else could he keep popping up around every corner? After the phone incident, Marcus had stopped carrying Grandpa's book around with him, just to be safe.

As he walked past the old playground where his dad had once brought him to do pull-ups—before it became painfully clear that Marcus would never be anything but skinny and unathletic—his phone beeped in his bag.

Marcus held his breath and grabbed the phone from the side pocket where he'd hidden it. The Cajun rice had done wonders absorbing the water from the phone, but it had also made it smell like a spice rack.

He hoped it was a message from Eddie. Marcus and Lena

had spent all of lunch working on a list of everything they could remember about Connie's party so Eddie could re-create it. But it was Marcus's mom asking if he'd want to visit Grandpa Joe tonight.

Marcus accidentally breathed in the spices wafting off his phone and started to cough. He sucked in a breath of fresh air and typed back: Can't go tonight. Test tomorrow. After the crying incident at the nursing home yesterday, he doubted his dad would let him set foot in there again anyway. There'd been no more talk of getting him new running shoes, which should have been a relief. But it had only made his dad's disappointment in him even clearer.

He rounded the corner, holding his breath again, and let out a relieved sigh when he didn't see anyone in front of Caspar's house. He hurried his steps until he was practically running. If he kept this up, maybe he really would be able to jog three miles one day.

He was almost in the clear when he heard a sound that cut right into his soul. It was a cry so pitiful that Marcus knew he couldn't ignore it, not if he could do something to help.

With a glance over his shoulder at Caspar's house—which still looked empty—he went to the pond on the other side of the street and listened intently until he heard the cry again. It was coming from a nearby clump of bushes.

He pushed some branches aside and saw a pair of yellow eyes staring at him. It was a cat, an old skeletal thing with mangy fur. It didn't have a collar around its neck, and the wild look in its eyes made Marcus wonder if it was feral.

Suddenly, the world shifted, and Marcus could see the cat's soul barely clinging to its body, like a piece of dandelion fluff about to blow off its stem. Then the colors faded away, and the world went back to normal again.

Lena hadn't said anything about collecting animals' souls. He wasn't even sure if that was part of her job. But Marcus had no doubt that this cat wouldn't be alive for very long. He stood frozen for a minute, not sure what to do.

He remembered what Lena had told him about souls wandering aimlessly if they weren't collected at the right time. Did that mean he should collect the cat's soul and make sure that at least it would die peacefully?

No. He couldn't kill it, not even if it was already dying. But he had to help it somehow. He would bring it to the vet, he decided. Maybe it wasn't too late.

He slowly took off his jacket, careful not to make any sudden movements, and then reached out to wrap the cat in it. The creature tried to wriggle away, clearly afraid but too weak to run.

"I won't hurt you," Marcus whispered. "I promise." He kept

talking to it in a calm voice until finally he was able to wrap the jacket around it. Holding his breath, he picked up the cat and brought it slowly to his chest.

When it was cradled in his arms, still wriggling but not fighting him, Marcus slowly got to his feet. But before he could turn to go, a voice behind him made him freeze.

"Hey, Dumpus!" It was Caspar Brown's voice.

Marcus didn't turn around.

"Dumpus, are you deaf? How do you like your new nickname?"

Marcus still didn't turn around.

"Whatchya got there?" Caspar asked, coming up next to him. "Cool! Is that cat dead?"

"No," Marcus said, trying to back away. "I'm taking it to the vet so they can help it."

"What's the hurry?" Caspar grabbed a stick off the ground and went to prod at the cat just as it let out another pitiful sound.

"Leave it alone!" Marcus said.

Caspar stopped and looked at him, clearly surprised to hear Marcus raise his voice. "Why do you care?" he asked. "Is this your cat or something?"

The creature started struggling in his grasp again, and Marcus knew he had to get out of there. "Just let me go."

"Come on. I want to have some fun with it."

"No," Marcus cried. "Leave it alone!" Then he turned and tried to run away, but Caspar grabbed his shirt and yanked him back. As Marcus lost his balance, the cat let out a yowl. It fought out of Marcus's arms, scratching and clawing at his hands until he couldn't hold on any longer. Then it leaped onto the ground and darted into the bushes.

Marcus looked down at his scratched hands, realizing with horror that at some point during the struggle, his fingers had started glowing deep purple. Then he watched as the glow faded, as if his fingers had done their job.

"No," Marcus whispered in disbelief. "No!" What had he done? Was the cat dead now because of him?

"Aw, man. You let it go!" Caspar said, ducking into the bushes to go after it. But Marcus couldn't let that happen.

"I said, leave it alone!" Marcus yelled, shoving Caspar aside.

The minute he did it, he knew he'd made a mistake. Not only was it crazy for him to touch anyone after his fingers had just been glowing, but Caspar seemed to double in size right before his eyes.

Marcus tried to turn, tried to run, but he wasn't quick enough to get away.

chapter 18

Marcus could barely see straight when he flopped onto his bed. It felt like his eyes were the wrong shape, like someone had dented them. He supposed Caspar's fists had done that...and more.

Every inch of him hurt so badly that he never wanted to move again. But he knew things were only going to get worse once his parents found out what had happened.

A little while later, there was a knock on his door. "Marcus?" his mom called. "We picked up some dinner on the way home. Come eat."

"I'm not hungry," he called, his voice barely more than a groan.

"What was that, honey?" she asked. Then she tried to open the door. "Why is this door locked? You know the rules. Open up."

"I-I can't."

"Marcus, open this door right now. I'm not joking."

It was no use. There was no way to hide this from his parents. Maybe if he explained things to his mom first, she'd get his dad to go easy on him.

He sighed and forced himself to sit up, every inch of his body creaking like it was made of old wood. Then he stumbled to the door and pulled it open.

His mom took one look at him and screamed. "What happened to you?"

"Nothing," he said. "I got into a fight."

"A fight? What fight? Who were you fighting with?"

"I wasn't fighting anyone. The guy was fighting me."

"But why?"

"There was a cat and I was trying to save it and…" Marcus shook his head. Even if he could explain what had really happened, his mom wouldn't believe him.

"This is ridiculous. I'm calling the school—"

"No, Mom!" he said. "This wasn't at school."

"Then where was it? And who did this to you? Who?"

This was it, his chance to turn Caspar in and get him in trouble. Then maybe all of Marcus's problems with the dumb bully would be over.

But before he could say anything, his dad appeared in the doorway. "What the heck happened to you?"

"He said he got into a fight over a cat," his mom said.

"A cat? Why on earth were you fighting about a cat?"

Marcus shrugged, figuring it was better not to try to explain.

"Did you throw the first punch or did he?" his dad asked. It figured that he'd care about something like that.

Marcus thought back. "I guess I did," he said finally. "I mean, I pushed him. After that, it was kind of a blur."

"So let me get this straight," his dad said. "You pushed him once, and then he did this to you? And you stood there and took it?"

"He attacked me. Then he—"

"And not once did you try to defend yourself? Not once did you fight back? Haven't I taught you anything?"

"I did what you wanted!" Marcus cried. "You're always telling me to stand up for myself. I tried, and it didn't work, okay?"

"Marcus, your father is not condoning violence," his mom broke in, which was laughable since that's *exactly* what he was doing. "But if you're going to provoke a boy, then you need to be ready for the consequences."

Marcus couldn't believe it. "Are you saying I deserved to get beaten up?"

"No, of course not," his mom said, but the look on his dad's face told him differently.

"Get yourself cleaned up," he told Marcus. "Then come eat dinner."

"I'm not hungry."

His dad puckered his mouth so the scar underneath it—a "souvenir" from his hockey days—looked even whiter than usual. "Hungry or not, it's dinnertime. So you're going to come to the table and sit with us until we tell you that you can go. Understood?" He stormed out of the room without another word.

His mom gave Marcus a sad smile. "I know he's tough on you," she said softly, "but it's his way of showing you that he cares." She tried to brush Marcus's hair away from his bruised cheek, but he flinched away. "Promise me you won't get into any more fights, okay?"

That was an easy promise to make. Marcus never wanted to feel this way again. "Okay."

She gave him one last pitying look and left him alone.

A second later, Ann-Marie appeared in the doorway. "What happened to you?" she asked. "Did you get thrown in a trash compactor or something?"

Marcus flopped back on his bed. "No, but I spent all day smelling like trash. Just like Mom." In fact, he probably still smelled terrible since he hadn't had a chance to change out of his garbage clothes.

He waited for his sister to make fun of him or to tell him that he should have stood up for himself like his dad had. Instead, she ducked out of the room and came back a minute later with a bag of frozen Brussels sprouts. "Put these on your face," she said. "It'll bring the swelling down."

"Thanks." It figured that Ann-Marie would even be the perfect sister when he was hurt, but he couldn't hate her for it at the moment. He was just glad that someone in his family wasn't counting how many punches he'd managed to get in before Caspar had kicked his butt.

He expected Ann-Marie to leave, so he was startled when she sat on the bed beside him and said, "I'm worried about Grandpa Joe."

Her voice was low and sad. Marcus and Grandpa had always been so close that he sometimes forgot that Ann-Marie loved him too, in her own way.

"Why did he have to get sick?" she went on. "First Grandma Lily and now him. It's not fair. Dad's parents are the worst, and they never even get colds. They'll be around forever!"

Marcus had to laugh, although it hurt his ribs. "Remember last year when they made us eat eel on Christmas? Who eats *eel*?"

She giggled. "It was like eating a shoe. Except at least a shoe smells better!"

They both laughed again, and then finally they fell quiet. "I miss having him around," she whispered, and he knew she was talking about Grandpa again.

"I know," Marcus said. "I do too. But he'll be okay." The words sounded like a lie as they came out of his mouth. And when he glanced over at Ann-Marie, he could tell that she had heard it too.

chapter 19

"Lena!" Hayleigh said at lunch the next day. "Abigail and I had the best idea!"

"What is it?" Lena asked, slowly unwrapping her sandwich. She knew better than to get excited about Hayleigh's ideas. A lot of times they involved glue guns.

"I know you usually do props and sets for the play," Hayleigh said, "but what if you did costumes with me this year? You're really good at sewing because of all that quilting stuff you do, and that way, we'll all get to be together."

Lena forced herself to smile. "Thanks, but I don't think I can do backstage this time."

"What?" Abigail exclaimed. "But you always do the play."

"I'm too busy this year." With everything going on with her dad and her powers, she had enough to think about. But if she were being honest with herself, it was more than that. Lena was happy for Abigail—she really was—but she couldn't stand to go to play practice and see her onstage while she sorted through smelly old costumes.

"Is this because of Marcus?" Abigail asked.

Lena swallowed. "What do you mean?" Had her friends noticed that something strange was going on?

"I know you said you're not together or anything, but you've been spending a lot of time with him."

"Yeah," Hayleigh chimed in. "I saw you with him in the hallway yesterday during homeroom." She giggled. "I was spying on you guys through that little window on the door."

"We were only out there because of Brent Adamson," Lena said. "He was sick. We were trying to help him."

Abigail laughed. "Oh yeah! I heard he threw up in gym this morning and had to go home again."

Poor Brent. He'd taken one look at Lena during volleyball and gotten sick all over his sneakers. She really hoped the hex she'd accidentally put on him wore off soon, or one of them would need to switch classes.

"But seriously, Lena," Abigail went on. "If there's something going on with you and Marcus, you can tell us. I mean, you did kiss him and everything."

Lena felt her cheeks get even redder. If only her friends knew how many times she and Marcus had actually kissed. Not that any of those times actually meant anything.

"He's had a crush on you since forever," Hayleigh said. "Remember when he kept drooling over you last year during that math project? No wonder you had to do all the work."

"He wasn't drooling! And he did lots of work. He didn't talk much during our presentation because he's shy."

"Yeah, right," Hayleigh said. "I don't know why he didn't ask you out last year. Maybe he was afraid you'd say no."

Lena opened her mouth and closed it again. What if Marcus *had* asked her on a date last year after their math project was over? What would she have said? And would the answer be different if he were to ask her out now?

She shook her head, trying to clear it of all those pesky, confusing questions. "You guys know how I feel about all that mushy stuff."

Abigail rolled her eyes. "Just because your dad keeps drilling anti-love things into your head, it doesn't mean they're true."

"Of course they're true. It's science!"

"So does that mean me liking Emery Higgins isn't for real?" Hayleigh asked.

Abigail's mouth fell open. "Since when do you like Emery? What about his braces?"

"You know I like shiny things," Hayleigh said, waggling her eyebrows. "And he helped me clean my locker after some puffy paint exploded in it yesterday. He's nice." She turned to Lena. "Are you saying that's all fake?"

"Yes," Lena said, but she could hear the doubt in her own voice. She wasn't sure what was true anymore. After everything that had happened the past few days, she was starting to wonder if there *were* things that science couldn't explain. And Hayleigh seemed happy as she started babbling on about how sweet Emery was. Who was Lena to take that away from her? In fact, part of her was a little jealous. What would it be like to let yourself feel that way about someone without worrying that it was all a lie?

She found herself scanning the cafeteria for Marcus, but she couldn't find him. She wasn't sure where he ate lunch now that Pradeep had moved away. Come to think of it, she hadn't seen Marcus all day, not even in math.

She grabbed her phone to send him a message, but she saw that there was one waiting for her from Eddie.

Good news, kid, it said. The party is on for this Friday. Same time and place.

She couldn't believe it. Eddie had come through! She only had to survive the rest of the week, and then everything would go back to normal.

That's great! she wrote back.

A minute later, her phone beeped again. Just in time too, Eddie had written. *We have been getting reports of failed matches and stubborn souls all day. The sooner we get you two back to normal, the better.*

Lena swallowed. How many of those failed matches and souls not wanting to leave their bodies were her fault? Zapping her dad had been an accident, but she'd known that using her power on Brent Adamson was a bad idea and she'd done it anyway. All of Eddie's talk about the balance of the universe had sounded hokey, but maybe there was more truth to it than she'd realized. The longer their powers stayed swapped, the harder it would be to make everything right again, not just for her and Marcus but for everyone.

Lena was soggy from the rain by the time she pulled her bike up to Marcus's house and knocked on the door. She'd looked for him all day at school and finally figured he must have stayed home sick.

As she waited for someone to open the door, Lena realized she'd never been inside Marcus's house. When they'd worked on their math project together, he'd always insisted they meet at her place. One time, she'd had to drop some papers off at his house, but he hadn't let her get past the porch, almost like he was embarrassed to let her in.

When the door finally creaked open, Lena stared in shock at the bruised face peering back at her. "Marcus? What happened?"

"Long story. What are you doing here?"

"I didn't know if you'd gotten Eddie's message. You said your phone wasn't working."

"Oh yeah. I got it." He didn't sound nearly as excited as she would have expected. In fact, he looked sad and droopy, like all the energy had been sucked out of him.

"It's good news, right?" she said. "Maybe the party really will switch things back." She decided not to mention the other stuff Eddie had told her. Judging by how he looked, she was pretty sure Marcus couldn't handle any bad news right now.

He only shrugged in response.

"Come on," she said. "What happened?"

"I had a disagreement with a meat grinder," Marcus said, but neither of them laughed.

"Can I come in?" Maybe if Lena could get him to sit down and talk to her, she could figure out what was going on.

But Marcus shook his head and said, "Um, my house is kind of a mess right now. How about we sit outside?"

"It's raining. Besides, I don't care about that. You should see how much fur is at my house. Professor's been shedding like crazy."

But Marcus was already out on the porch, shutting the door behind him. Now that he was outside, she could see how bad his face looked.

"Who did this to you?" she asked.

Instead of answering, he plopped down on the rickety porch swing, which was only half-protected from the rain by an awning. But Lena wasn't going to give up that easily.

She sat down next to him. "I won't judge or anything. Just tell me."

"Caspar Brown."

"That Neanderthal? Didn't he set a teacher's hair on fire last year? I forgot he even went to school with us."

"You probably never see him because he keeps getting suspended. But he lives down the street, so I run into him all the time."

"Why did he do this to you?"

"I was trying to keep him from attacking a cat, so he attacked me instead." Finally, he told her the whole story, about the cat, about his glowing fingers, about shoving Caspar. The words came out in a tumble, and the whole time, he kept his eyes closed like he didn't want to see who he was spilling his guts to.

"Wow," Lena said when he was done. "Do you think that means the power works on animals too?"

Marcus's eyes snapped open. "Don't you get it? I killed that cat!"

"You don't know that. You didn't actually see it die, did you?" He gave her a slight shake of his head. "So it could be okay. But if you did collect its soul, that means you helped it. It was almost dead anyway. And it was in pain."

"No," he said. "I tried to help it, and I did the opposite."

"Marcus, you didn't do anything wrong," she said slowly. "I'm the one who's messed up with my dad and with Brent. I'm the one who should have known better than to zap people. But what you did wasn't like that. You were trying to help."

They sat for a long moment in silence. Lena wasn't sure if what she'd said had gotten through to him, but he seemed calmer than before.

"You know what the craziest thing is?" he asked softly. "All day, I've been hearing meowing. At first I thought it was the neighbor's cat, but then I heard it when I was in the shower. As if I don't feel guilty enough!" He glanced at Lena. "You don't have to say it. I know I sound crazy."

She had to admit that what he'd said did sound crazy, but she wasn't about to say that to him. "Guilt does weird things to people," she said instead. "When I was little, I stole my mom's quilting shears and then lied about it. I had nightmares about getting chased by scissors two nights in a row. Finally, I woke my mom up in the middle of the night and confessed everything."

"I didn't think you had it in you to be a delinquent," Marcus said, cracking a smile.

Lena shrugged. "I was working on my first quilt, and the safety scissors my parents gave me were so dull that they were driving me crazy. I guess it's a good thing I didn't think to steal a steak knife or something."

This time Marcus actually laughed, his mood finally lightening. Then he turned to her with a curious look on his face. "You never talk about your mom. I think this is the first time I've ever heard you mention her."

Lena shrugged. "She left when I was in fifth grade."

"I kind of remember that. You didn't come to school for a couple of weeks, and we all thought you had the plague. I was expecting you to have pockmarks and stuff when you finally came back, but you just looked really sad."

Lena sighed, remembering. "I was so depressed that I couldn't get out of bed for two weeks. She moved out one day, no warning or anything. Funny how her job was all about helping sick people not be in pain, and then she left me and my dad just like that. She didn't care about hurting us."

"I'm sorry," Marcus said.

She hated the pitying look on his face. And the last thing she wanted to think about was her mom when everything else was already hard enough.

"What you did with the cat, it was brave, Marcus. You could have just left it there, but you did your best to help it."

Marcus let out a bitter laugh. "I wish my dad saw it that way. He thinks I'm the biggest loser ever born."

"You're not a loser."

"I don't have any friends," he said.

Lena looked at him and found herself saying, "I'm your friend." She realized it was true. Maybe she didn't know Marcus as well as she knew Abigail, but he felt like the only person she could trust right now. Plus, it hurt her to see him so upset. Somewhere along the way, she'd actually started to care about him.

He let out a long sigh. Then he got to his feet. "Do you want to come inside? I want to show you something."

chapter 20

Marcus had never let anyone from school into his house, not even Pradeep. But for some reason, he needed Lena to see what things in his life were really like. He needed her to understand it all. If she still wanted to be friends with him after that, then he'd know that he really could trust her.

He opened the front door of his house and took a deep breath before going inside. As Lena trailed after him, he tried to see the living room through her eyes.

The space was stuffed full of gym equipment and trophies. Everywhere you looked, his sister's face was staring back at you. There was even a cardboard cutout of Ann-Marie propped up next to the fireplace, one that his dad had made last year to help cheer her on at a state meet.

"See?" he said softly, not looking at Lena. "I told you my house is a mess."

"Wow, these are all about your sister?" she asked, looking

at the slew of newspaper clippings that his dad had tacked up on the walls.

"Yeah. She's kind of a big deal around here, in case you can't tell. She was always good at everything, but the past couple of years, it's all my dad can think about. When he's not coaching the high school hockey team, he spends every second training with her. Most of the time, it's like I don't exist. I mean, there aren't even any pictures of me anymore! My room's the only place in the whole house that's not full of track stuff. Except for the basement, but that's crammed with garbage for my mom's junk sculptures." He laughed bitterly. "I live with a bunch of crazy people."

He'd never said any of this aloud to anyone before. It felt strange but good somehow, like he was airing out a room that had been locked up for years.

"Is this why you don't let anyone come over?" Lena asked.

"Would you invite people to your house if it looked like this?"

"Probably not," she admitted, and he was actually glad to hear her be honest. He'd been afraid she'd try to tell him it wasn't that bad, but it *was* bad. There was no hiding it. He could see Lena crinkling her nose at the trash smell wafting from the basement.

"Do you still want to hang out in here?" he asked. "Isn't it better to be out in the rain?"

But Lena didn't seem to be listening. Instead, she walked from trophy to trophy, reading the inscriptions on the bottom. "That must be hard," she said finally. "Everywhere you look, you're reminded of your sister's accomplishments."

Marcus nodded. That's exactly how it felt. "And that I'll never be as good as her."

"You'll never *be* her," Lena corrected, "but that's good. Families should have variety. It's the most normal thing in the world. We would have never evolved without it." She turned to him. "Can I see your room?"

"Um, sure," he said, leading her down the hallway. It was weird to bring a girl into his room, but everything these days was weird. "I don't know how you can be so logical all the time. Don't things ever bother you?"

Lena blinked at him. "What? Of course things bother me."

"But you're so okay with everything. I mean, even this whole power-swapping mess. I've been freaking out the past few days, but you keep going along like everything's fine."

"Marcus," she said as she leaned against his desk, "didn't I just tell you that I couldn't get out of bed for two weeks after my mom left? I don't think that means things don't bother me."

Marcus perched on the edge of his bed, glad he'd remembered to make it that morning. "But what about since then? Do you ever get really angry or really upset?"

She seemed to think this over for a minute. "Not really. I guess there's no point."

Marcus shook his head. "Point or not, how can you not feel that stuff? All I do is feel things, even if I don't want to. I mean, I cried when my turtle died a few weeks ago!"

He couldn't believe he'd admitted that to someone, especially to the girl he liked. But Lena didn't judge him. Instead she smiled and said, "That must have been some turtle."

"He was the best. He could read." Marcus laughed at the incredulous look on her face. "I'm serious! He would chew up the newspapers I gave him and leave whole articles intact. I think those were the ones he liked."

"That sounds like Professor," Lena said. "My dog only barks when people on TV speak French. I'm convinced he can understand them."

"You believe in that kind of thing? I would think you'd be looking for some scientific explanation."

"There probably is one, but I'm starting to think that I don't always have to know what that is." She went over to Marcus's model collection. "What's this?"

"Oh, um, nothing. Just a hobby."

She picked up the lunar module and smiled. He waited for her to make fun of his collection like some of Pradeep's friends had when he'd brought in an old rocket ship to show them during gym class last year, but all she said was, "My dad would love this. He's totally into space stuff."

And that was it. She didn't tease him or tell him he was wasting his time. She simply accepted this as another thing about him and kept examining his collection.

"This is great!" she said after a minute, spotting the moon ship on his worktable. "Are you putting it together?"

"I'm trying to fix it. There's one piece I still can't find, but I think I might be able to take it out of one of my other models. I wouldn't normally do that, but I want to get this done for my..." Marcus trailed off. He couldn't tell her about Grandpa, not yet.

As if she could read his mind, at that moment, Lena spotted Grandpa Joe's dating book on his desk. "What's this?"

"Nothing!" Marcus jumped up to grab it, but Lena was already flipping through.

"Why is a bunch of this stuff highlighted? *Always bring a girl flowers? Always pay her a compliment.*" She chuckled. "This is hilarious! And what are all these notes written in the margins?"

"It's nothing, okay?" he said, finally managing to snatch it away from her. "Just a book my grandpa gave me before he got sick." How much had she seen? Would she realize that the scribbles in the margins were about him trying to get her to notice him?

Lena's smile faded. "Is your grandpa okay?"

Marcus slammed the book shut. He might have been able to confide in Lena about the cat and his weird family, but if he told her about Grandpa Joe, he was afraid she'd launch into her scientific explanations about life and death. He couldn't deal with that. All he wanted, suddenly, was to be left alone.

"He's fine. Sorry, but you should probably go. I have homework I need to do."

"But—"

He marched out into the hall. "Thanks for coming over. I'll see you at school tomorrow, if my dad lets me out of the house. He said I looked too pathetic to go anywhere today."

"Marcus, I'm sorry," Lena said, trailing after him as he marched toward the front door. "I shouldn't have touched your stuff."

"It's okay." Suddenly he felt bad about practically shoving her out the door. "I'll see you tomorrow, okay?"

She nodded and let herself out, leaving Marcus standing alone in the cluttered hallway.

chapter 21

As Lena pedaled home from Marcus's house, she tried to figure out what she'd done wrong. Maybe she shouldn't have touched the dating book, but why did Marcus care so much about that old thing? She was pretty sure it was the one she'd seen him with at Connie Reynolds's party the other night.

She was also pretty sure she'd seen her own name scrawled in the margins. But why would Marcus have written about her in an old book on dating?

Were her friends right? Did Marcus like her after all? The thought sent her stomach fluttering so much that Lena wondered if she'd accidentally swallowed a bug. Then again, guys who liked you didn't usually kick you out of their houses.

When she got home, Lena was surprised to see her dad's car sitting in the driveway again. Since when did he take two afternoons off in a row?

She opened the door to the smell of burning. "What's going on?" she cried over the loud music blaring through the house.

"I'm making dinner!" he said as smoke billowed up from a frying pan.

Lena rushed over and turned off the burner. There were charred bits of something in the pan that might have once been pieces of chicken.

Dad chuckled as he fanned the air with a dish towel. "I guess I'm a little rusty. It's been a while since I cooked."

Lena swallowed. Years ago, before her mom left, she and her parents had spent weekend afternoons cooking together. Her mom had had Lena peel vegetables while she and Dad had chopped and seasoned things. On those days, the dark cloud that seemed to always hang over Mom's head would disappear, at least for a few hours.

"What's the occasion?" Lena asked.

Her dad gave her a sad smile. "It was supposed to be dinner for Marguerite, but she canceled. She said we'd reschedule, but to be honest...I'm not sure she wants to see me again."

"What? But things seemed fine yesterday." Was it possible the spark had faded and that things would finally go back to normal?

Dad shrugged. "I thought they were. But when she called today, she sounded different. She claimed she was sick, but I suspect that was an excuse to get out of seeing me again." He laughed, but Lena could hear the sadness underneath it.

"Where's Professor?" she asked, realizing the dog hadn't greeted her at the door with his usual unappealing gift.

"Oh, he's staring out the window as always. There's a squirrel in the yard that seems to have taken a fancy to him. They've been making eyes at each other all afternoon."

Her dad chuckled, but Lena's stomach went cold. As she approached the back door, sure enough, there was Professor with his nose pressed up against the glass. And on the other side, looking equally intent, was a small gray squirrel. Their gazes were locked like they couldn't bear to look away from each other.

Oh no.

"Professor?" Lena asked softly, but his ears didn't even move at the sound of his name.

Lena's mind raced. Had she accidentally zapped Professor and not realized it? But that was impossible. She hadn't touched him since she'd realized her powers were on the fritz. Except… She thought back to when her dad and Marguerite had left the house yesterday, and she'd sat staring out the window after them for a long time. Had Professor come over to be petted? She couldn't remember, but it was exactly the kind of thing he would have done. And in her distracted state of mind, she very well could have touched him without realizing it.

And now here he was, drooling over a squirrel not because he wanted to eat it but because he wanted to have little half-dog/half-squirrel babies with it. Great.

"I'm sorry, boy," Lena said, but he ignored her and gave a little whine as he pawed at the glass. The squirrel did the same on the other side. Two star-crossed lovers straight out of *Romeo and Juliet*. When she'd read the play in school, Lena had found the whole story ridiculous, but it was nothing compared to what was happening before her eyes.

Lena sighed and slid open the glass door. The moment it was open, Professor bounded outside and touched his nose to the squirrel's. Lena could practically feel the sparks flying between them, even if she couldn't see them at that moment. Then the two creatures started running around the yard together in a way that Lena could only describe as "frolicking." Ew.

She sighed again and went back to helping her dad clean up the kitchen. As she watched him absently scrubbing the burnt pan, her vision shifted, and she could see the gray aura surrounding him again. This time, she knew the loneliness was her fault. If she hadn't zapped him in the first place, her dad wouldn't be so bummed about getting ditched.

"Dad, I'm sorry about this whole Marguerite thing," Lena

said. Then she spotted something in the gray haze, a hint of a spark buzzing around him. The love jolt wasn't completely gone, at least not on his side. Maybe he needed to go see Marguerite and rekindle it a little.

Lena blinked. She couldn't believe she was thinking of encouraging her dad to keep this whole mess going, but the sadness was so thick around him now when only yesterday it had seemed like it was gone. If there was a chance he really could be happy with Marguerite, she couldn't keep it from happening, could she?

"Dad, I know what we should do. If Marguerite's sick, we should bring her some soup. Then she'll remember how awesome you are."

"Do you think so?"

"Yeah, we can stop at that soup place on Main Street."

He gave her a long look. "And you want to come too? I can't tell you how happy I am that you're so understanding about all of this, Chipmunk. I know since your mom's been gone, things have been hard…on both of us. I didn't want to rush into anything in case you weren't all right with it."

"I know. But it's okay. Really."

Something in her voice must have sounded convincing because her dad grabbed his car keys. "Where's Professor?" he asked.

"Oh, um, I think he'll be happier out in the yard while we're gone," she said, heading for the car.

After they'd picked up some chicken noodle soup, they drove to Marguerite's town house. Dad parked the car and then called Marguerite to let her know they were outside her door.

"We thought we'd surprise you with some soup. Maybe we could all watch a movie?" He listened for a minute. "Lena's with me. That's okay, right?"

Lena realized that her coming along might not have been the best way to get these two to rekindle things, but what if seeing each other wasn't enough? What if Marguerite needed another zap? Lena knew she shouldn't risk it—especially after what Eddie had told her about their swapped powers affecting other people's assignments—but if she had a chance to see her dad happy again, she had to take it. She would worry about the balance of the universe once her dad was okay.

Finally, Dad hung up. "It took some convincing," he told Lena, "but we're in!"

As they headed up the walkway, Lena got her energy ready to go just in case. She walked behind her dad so he wouldn't notice her fingers glowing.

The minute Marguerite opened the door, Lena could see that the spark inside her was totally gone. No wonder she hadn't wanted to see Dad again. But one more zap would fix that.

Before Marguerite could even say hello, Lena ducked around her dad and brushed the woman's arm with her fingers. Then she stepped back and waited.

The transformation happened immediately. Marguerite's face went from hesitant to overjoyed.

"I can't believe you did this!" she cried, taking the soup from Dad's hands.

"It was my pleasure," he said, his eyes suddenly dreamy.

As the two of them stood chatting and laughing in the doorway, it was clear they'd forgotten all about Lena. That was fine with her. They were happy. That was all that mattered. And she had to admit that seeing them that way made her wish, just for a minute, that she could have someone to laugh with too.

Lena shook that thought out of her head and decided to sneak away before either of them noticed. Then she started on the long walk home.

chapter 22

Marcus crept into school the next morning with a baseball cap pulled low over his eyes. He knew a teacher would tell him to take it off any second, but at least that would give him a little more time without anyone noticing his bruises. It also meant Caspar Brown might not zero in on him right away.

When he got to his locker, he found Lena waiting for him. If this kept up, people would start thinking she was his girlfriend. A little thrill went through him at the thought, but he had to play it cool. *Don't look too eager*, Grandpa's book was always saying. For all he knew, she still had her eye on Brent Adamson.

"Hey," she said. "How are you feeling?"

"Like a bruised pear, but otherwise okay." He glanced around and then reluctantly pulled his baseball cap off and shoved it in his locker. No one gasped in horror, so maybe he didn't look too bad. Or, more likely, no one cared enough to actually look at him.

"I made this for you," Lena said, pulling a piece of quilted flannel out of her backpack. "It's a cover for your book. That way it won't get more damaged."

"Wow, thanks." He couldn't believe that Lena had taken all that time to make him a present.

"I'm sorry I touched the book," she said. "It obviously means a lot to you."

He shook his head. "It wasn't about that. It was…" It was Grandpa, but he couldn't tell her about that. Not here, in the middle of the hallway.

"Oh, and I brought you something else." She took what looked like a math book out of her bag. "Take this manual home and memorize it, and make sure to bring yours for me tomorrow so I can read it."

He looked down at the soul-collecting manual and frowned. "I didn't expect it to look so normal."

"Did you think it would be wrapped in human skin or something?" Lena asked with a soft laugh. "What's your manual look like?"

"Pretty much like this one," he admitted. "Still, I thought the death one would look different." He hesitated for another moment before finally taking the book from Lena's hands.

"You're really freaked out by death, huh?" Lena said.

He gave her a sharp look. "What? No!" He cleared his throat. "I mean, isn't everyone?"

She shrugged. "Not me. I guess that's why they wanted me for this job. I'm a weirdo."

"You're not a weirdo," Marcus said. "I think you're... It's amazing that you can handle it all so well. I wish I could do that."

She shrugged again, but he could tell by the way her cheeks turned slightly pink that she was flattered. "I've been thinking," she said. "Maybe we should meet up after school and coach each other on our powers. I mean, who knows how long we'll be stuck with them?"

"But what about the party tomorrow? Connie's acting like she's been planning it for weeks even though Eddie planted the idea in her head yesterday. If he can do that, then the rest of the plan will have to work, won't it?"

Lena sighed. "I hope so. But if it doesn't, at some point Eddie's boss will get sick of waiting and start giving us assignments again. I figure we should be ready."

"Assignments? But...but I can't take anyone's soul." He'd spent all of last night having nightmares about the old cat, and every once in a while, he could still hear a phantom meow nearby. He couldn't go through that again, especially not with a person!

"You probably won't have to," she said, "but it's a good idea to be prepared, just in case. Right?"

"Why are you so eager to learn this stuff? I thought this whole matchmaking thing was a big joke to you."

Lena ran her finger along the edge of a nearby locker, not meeting his eyes. "Maybe…maybe it's not as silly as I thought at first. My dad's been a lot happier lately because of it."

"So the spark between him and that woman hasn't faded?" Marcus had figured a match that hadn't been an actual assignment would probably fizzle out after a day or two.

"Well, it did," Lena said slowly. "So I recharged it a little."

"You *what*?" Marcus cried. Then he looked around, realizing kids were staring at them. He ducked his head and whispered, "Why would you do that?"

"You should have seen how sad my dad was when Marguerite started ignoring him. I had to do something."

"But rezapping could make things worse! If it turns out they're not a love match, when the spark fades, your dad will come crashing down and be even more miserable."

Lena's face paled. "See, this is why I need your help! Then I can stop doing dumb things like making my dog fall in love with a squirrel."

Marcus let out a startled laugh. "Your dog did what?"

Lena shook her head. "Don't ask. It's so embarrassing. I saw him gathering nuts this morning." He laughed again, which finally made her smile a little. "I guess it is kind of funny. But

I can't keep doing stuff like that. So will you meet me after school today or not?"

"All right, I'll help you," Marcus said. Who knew how much she'd want to hang out with him after Eddie found a way to swap their powers back? She might kiss him one more time at the party tomorrow night and then—zap—never speak to him again.

The thought stabbed at him. Before he and Lena had started spending so much time together, he'd been consumed with getting her to notice him. But now that they were friends, his feelings felt like more than just a crush. The truth was, now that Grandpa Joe was sick, she was the only person he could really talk to.

"Okay. Meet me in the back field after school," Lena said. Then she gave him another smile and hurried down the hall.

Marcus's heart lifted. He didn't need to consult Grandpa's book to know what had just happened. He and Lena had finally planned their first date.

chapter 23

The back field wasn't even really a field. It was more of a swamp on which kids sometimes had to play soccer during gym class. As Lena waited for Marcus to meet her for the second day in a row, she spotted Brent Adamson and a couple of his friends cutting across the field on their way home.

As Brent turned his head toward her, Lena could tell the exact moment when he caught sight of her. He froze in his tracks, leaned over, and threw up all over the grass. His friends jumped away from him as if he'd turned radioactive.

Lena quickly ducked behind the bleachers so he wouldn't see her anymore. She kept hoping that the spell on Brent would fade, but until then, she'd have to keep trying to stay out of sight.

Funnily enough, even if everything got reversed at Connie's party tonight and Lena could start focusing on her coming-of-age checklist again, she had to admit that she had no interest in kissing Brent or going on a date with him anymore. Not when she'd seen so much disgusting stuff coming out of his plump lips.

In fact, she was starting to wonder if kissing Brent would have been nearly as nice as kissing Marcus had been. Even if that kiss in Connie Reynolds's closet had been the first step to a whole disastrous roller coaster, it *had* been pretty nice. Despite all the crazy stuff that had happened the past few days, she was glad she'd gotten to know Marcus better. There was a lot more to him than the shy, awkward guy she'd known since elementary school.

Her cheeks started to burn as she spotted Marcus coming toward her across the field. Would he be able to tell by the look on her face that she'd been thinking about him?

Just in case, she grabbed the large plastic bag she'd brought and shoved it at him. "I made this for you. Or really, for your grandpa. I figured it might be cold at the nursing home." After he'd finally told her about his grandpa being sick yesterday after school, Lena had been desperate to do something to help. Finally, she'd started working on a blue-and-white quilt with an intricate pattern that made her think of constellations.

"Wow, thanks. You made this in one night?" he asked.

Lena shrugged. "If I'd done it by hand, it would have taken longer, but with a sewing machine, it's not so bad."

"You're really good at this quilting stuff, huh?" he said.

She shrugged and plucked a blade of grass. "My mom taught me when I was little. We used to make them together. I guess I'm just in the habit now."

"Do you ever get to see your mom?" he asked.

"She comes to visit around Christmas, but that usually makes things worse. It always makes my dad depressed." Lena wound the grass around her finger. "Maybe this year, if my dad and Marguerite are still together, it won't be so bad. I've been meaning to ask you. How often would I have to zap my dad to keep him happy?"

Marcus gawked at her. "You're going to do it again? I told you that it could make everything worse."

"I'm not saying I *will* do it," she said, casting the piece of grass aside. "But I want to know, in case I have to." She couldn't let her dad's gray aura come back dark and thick like it had been. Now that she knew it was there, she couldn't pretend it wasn't, not even after her powers went back to normal.

Marcus sighed and pulled a book out of his bag. "Here's the matchmaking manual. It should explain everything. Basically, if the spark is still strong in one of the people, then sometimes if they spend more time together, you don't have to do anything. But if the spark goes out in both of them, you're pretty much starting from scratch." His forehead wrinkled. "Are you sure your dad and this woman are meant to be together?"

"Like soul mates?" Lena snorted. Then she saw the hurt look on Marcus's face. "Sorry. They're both scientists, they like the same kind of food, and they even watch the same boring old TV shows. That has to mean they're a good match, right?"

"It depends. Common interests are good, but then there's the whole 'opposites attract' theory. You never really know what makes people click."

She sighed. "I guess I'll try to make them spend a lot of time together and hopefully they'll grow on each other. Okay, your turn."

"My turn?" Marcus looked at her in alarm.

"Yeah, what do you want to know about soul collecting? Did you read the manual I gave you?"

"Um, not yet. To be honest, I've been kind of distracted. I still keep hearing a cat meowing."

Lena frowned. "Really? Do you hear it now?"

Marcus sat down on the grass and seemed to listen for a moment. "There!" he said finally, pointing to some bushes near the bleachers. "It's like it's haunting me!"

For a second, Lena thought she could hear a faint sound too. Then it faded away. She chewed on her lip thoughtfully.

"I guess it's possible," she said slowly. "Tell me again what happened when you took its soul."

He sighed and started going over the details again. When he got to the part about realizing his fingers were glowing, Lena held up her hand. "Wait," she said. "So your energy didn't disappear into the cat, right? Your fingers were still glowing after it ran into the bushes?"

"Um, I guess so. I don't really remember."

"That explains it! You didn't totally release its soul. You only gave it a little nudge. Maybe that means it's still alive. But it was so sick when you found it, it probably didn't have long anyway." Lena gasped as she suddenly noticed the ground next to him. "Um, Marcus?"

He glanced down and yelped at the sight of a perfect circle of dead grass that had formed around him. Meanwhile, the rest of the field was still bright green.

"This is crazy!" he said, jumping to his feet. "I can't go around killings things."

"Marcus," Lena said, reaching out to put her hand on his shoulder.

"Don't touch me!" he cried. "Do you want me to hurt you too?"

"Whoa." Lena held up her hands in surrender. Obviously, he wanted to be left alone. So she wandered away and slowly approached the bushes near the bleachers where Marcus had heard meowing. She bent down and made little clicking noises with her tongue, holding her hand out like she was offering the creature a treat.

She held her breath as the bushes seemed to rustle a little. And then, something emerged from them. It wasn't a cat. It wasn't even really a thing. It was more like a glimmer of light shimmering through the air. She could tell by Marcus's wide eyes that he could see it too.

chapter 24

Marcus stared at the glowing ghost cat. Then he suddenly found himself laughing with relief. He'd been so worried that he'd accidentally killed the creature, it hadn't occurred to him that its soul might still be around. Lena was right. The cat wouldn't have lived long after he'd found it. He'd tried to help it and he'd failed, but maybe he was being given a second chance now.

"Come here, kitty," he said softly, making clicking sounds like he'd heard Lena do. The little ball of light seemed to take a couple of hesitant steps toward him.

Then Marcus's phone started to ring, and the flicker of light disappeared back into the shrubbery.

Marcus sighed and pulled the phone out of his bag. He plugged up his nose so he wouldn't smell the Cajun spices and answered it.

"Eddie, I was just thinking I should call you," he said

through his nose. "What can you tell me about ghost animals? I'm pretty sure I have a ghost cat following me around. How do I help it?"

"A ghost cat?" Eddie chuckled. "That is not something you hear every day. Well, animal souls are different from human souls. They don't need someone to send them to the After. The cat's soul will stay around until it gets bored, and then it will curl up somewhere and move on. Easy as that."

"Really?" Marcus's chest lightened. He hadn't doomed the cat to an eternity of wandering the world as a ghost.

"But listen, kid," Eddie said, his voice growing oddly quiet. "Have you got a minute?"

"Um, sure," Marcus said. He held his phone away for a second so he could suck in a breath of nonspicy air.

"You okay? You sound funny."

"Yup!"

"So look," Eddie said, his words slow and careful. "I have an assignment for you today. A soul collection."

"What? But you said I wouldn't have to do any of those."

"I know, kid, but the boss lady is losing patience. I'll send you the details, but…" He cleared his throat. "Look, I am sorry about this. I wish it didn't have to be this way." Then, before Marcus could say anything else, he hung up the phone.

"Eddie!" Marcus called, his hand falling away from his nose.

Instantly, the spicy smell shot up his nostrils, and he started to cough.

"What happened?" Lena asked.

"Eddie said"—*cough!*—"I have to"—*cough!*—"do a collection." *Cough!* After he'd shoved the phone in his pocket, the coughing attack finally faded. "He said he was sorry, but I don't care how sorry he is. I'm not going to do it!"

"If it's a sleeper, it might not be that bad," Lena said. "The person doesn't even know what's happening."

Just then, Marcus's phone beeped, and he glanced at it, keeping it as far away from his face as possible. He expected it to be a message from Eddie, but it was one from his mom: Grandpa is in the hospital. Can you get here right away?

Marcus gasped.

"What is it?" Lena asked.

He couldn't speak. Instead, he showed her the message, his hands shaking. He'd known this moment was coming— dreaded it—but that hadn't prepared him for how much it hurt.

His phone beeped again. This time it was a message from Eddie with the information about his new assignment.

The address of the hospital flashed across the screen. And then a name, one Marcus knew all too well. Joseph Marcus Fierro.

Grandpa Joe.

chapter 25

Marcus was still in a daze as he and Lena made a quick stop at his house before heading to the hospital. His parents had wanted him to come right away, but he'd had to pick up the moon ship first. He'd finally finished the model last night, deciding to take a piece from one of his other ones to complete it. Almost as if he'd known that he was running out of time. He also slipped Grandpa's book into his pocket, knowing its presence would make him feel better.

As they hurried toward the hospital, he glanced at the time and sucked in a breath. It had been more than a half hour since his mom's message. He hoped Grandpa was still…

Marcus shook his head. No. He'd get to the hospital and see that Grandpa was fine and that the message Eddie had sent him was some kind of mistake.

He was so consumed by his thoughts that he barely noticed

they were passing by Caspar Brown's house. Then he heard that unmistakable ape voice.

"Hey, Dumpus!"

Lena started to turn around, but Marcus shook his head. "Keep walking," he said.

"Hey, where are you going?" Caspar called after them.

"Ignore him," Marcus muttered, but he couldn't help the sinking feeling inside him. Why had he gotten careless? If they'd gone a different way, they could have avoided this.

"You can't run from Caspar forever, you know," Lena said.

That was easy for her to say, but what was he supposed to do?

It seemed like they were finally safe when Marcus felt someone grab his jacket from behind. Caspar yanked him backward and spun him around. "Why are you ignoring me?" he asked. "I was just trying to talk to you."

"Well, he doesn't want to talk to *you*," Lena said.

Caspar laughed. "You're having your girlfriend stand up for you now? Does she go digging around in the trash with the rest of your family?"

"Shut up," Marcus said, but Caspar only laughed again. Then his eyes lit up.

"What's that in your pocket?" He snatched Grandpa Joe's book before Marcus could stop him.

"No!" Marcus cried.

"What kind of crappy book is this?" Caspar asked, leafing through it. "It's like a million years old."

"Be careful with that. It's an antique," Lena said.

Caspar's grin widened. Then he took a step toward the pond, and Marcus knew what was going to happen. His book was going to wind up at the bottom like his phone had, and no amount of spicy rice would ever make it okay again.

"No," Marcus said, his body suddenly pulsing with anger. No one was going to ruin Grandpa's book, no matter how enormous he was. He took a step forward onto the grass and then another. "Give that back now."

Caspar's grin only grew bigger. "Or what?"

Suddenly, Marcus heard a strange crackling sound coming from his feet. He glanced down to see that all the grass around him, every single blade, had shriveled up and died.

Caspar's smile vanished. "How did you do that?"

"I-I didn't," Marcus stammered, but it was too late to deny it. His secret—at least part of it—was out. Marcus's first instinct was to make a run for it. Maybe if he got far enough away, Caspar would think he'd imagined the whole thing. But one look at Caspar's face told him that the bully would never let him forget this.

"I knew you were some kind of freak,'" Caspar said, his gaze still on the dead grass around Marcus's feet.

Then something rustled in the bushes, and Marcus heard a pitiful meow. A second later, a ball of light darted out of the bushes and rushed at Caspar. The boy didn't see it coming, but as it collided with his leg, he howled as if he'd been zapped with electricity.

"What was that?" Caspar asked, jumping back. Then he whirled around, clearly trying to find his attacker.

Lena and Marcus exchanged looks as the cat turned back for another pass.

"If you keep messing with me," Marcus said, his voice sounding stronger in his ears than it ever had before, "you'll find out. Now give me the book back."

Caspar's eyes doubled in size, and he let the book drop to the ground. Lena scrambled to grab it off the concrete. Thanks to its new quilted cover, the book looked unharmed.

"You...you're such a..." But for once, Caspar couldn't seem to come up with an insult. And when the cat let out another yowl, Caspar yelped in fear and scurried back toward his house.

"Good kitty," Marcus whispered as he watched the bully's front door slam shut behind him.

At that moment, his phone started buzzing in his pocket, telling Marcus he was running out of time before his assignment. He swallowed the sick feeling in his throat and turned to Lena. Maybe she was right. Maybe it was time to stop running.

"Let's go," he said.

chapter 26

Lena stopped in the hospital lobby and glanced over to find Marcus frozen in front of the elevator. He'd been eerily quiet since their encounter with Caspar, but now he suddenly looked like a panicked animal.

"It'll be okay," she told him, pressing the elevator button.

"I can't do this!" he erupted. "I thought I could stop running from stuff, but this… It's too much, Lena. I can't!"

When the elevator door opened, Lena went inside, but Marcus didn't move. "You have to at least go see him, don't you?" she asked.

Marcus's shoulders drooped, but he followed after her. They came out on the fifth floor, directly in front of a room with the words "O. Monroe" written on a whiteboard by the door.

"Hey, look," Lena whispered. "Do you think that could be Olivia?"

They peered in, and sure enough, the young woman from

the park was lying unconscious on the bed. A mystery novel sat on the table beside Olivia's bed, as if someone had been coming by to read to her.

"She looks better," Marcus whispered.

Lena nodded. Even though the woman was still unconscious, she seemed to have more life to her than when she'd been rushed off in the ambulance.

As Marcus turned away, Lena thought she saw a hint of a love spark fluttering near Olivia's heart. But that was impossible, wasn't it? It must have been a trick of the light.

When they got to the end of the hall, Marcus froze again. "It'll be okay," Lena whispered. She watched him take in a shaky breath and then give a little nod of his head.

They went into the room to find Marcus's parents and his sister sitting by the hospital bed. An old, frail man was asleep in the bed, hooked up to wires and machines. Lena didn't need her soul-collecting powers to know that he didn't have much time left.

"Marcus, there you are," a man who had to be Marcus's father said. "What took you so long?"

"I had to stop at home to pick something up," he said. "Oh, um, everyone, this is Lena."

Normally, she would have felt awkward meeting a boy's parents, but that was the least of her worries right now. His family looked at Marcus with confused expressions on their faces. Most guys probably didn't bring girls to their dying grandfather's hospital beds.

"I'm here for moral support," Lena explained.

"She made Grandpa a quilt," Marcus said, pulling it out of his backpack.

"Thank you, Lena," his mom said with a tired but warm smile. She turned to Marcus. "Grandpa hasn't been awake since we got here. They don't know if he *will* wake up, honey. But they said there's a good chance he can hear us, so if there's anything you'd like to say to him, now's the time." She looped her arm through Ann-Marie's. "We've already said our good-byes."

Marcus nodded. "Can...can I have some time alone with him?"

"Of course," his mom said.

When Marcus's family was gone, he slowly walked to Grandpa Joe's bedside and spread the quilt out over him. When she'd been frantically working on it the night before, Lena had hoped that the quilt would bring Grandpa Joe some comfort, but it seemed that Marcus was the one who needed comfort now.

"What do I do?" he asked Lena when he was done.

"Talk to him," she said. "Let him know you're here and that you'll make sure he'll be okay."

He nodded, but she could tell that he was still hesitant. "Do you want me to go?" she added. Maybe it would be easier for him to do this without her watching.

"No! Please stay. I can't do this by myself."

"Okay. I'll be right here."

He took a long breath and sat down beside the bed. "Hey," he said softly. "Um, I'm here, Grandpa. It's Marcus. I'm sorry I couldn't come sooner. I'm sorry I've barely come to see you at all these past few weeks. I was scared." He laughed softly. "I still am scared, but I'm here."

He glanced at Lena, as if looking for reassurance that he was doing things right. "Keep going," she said.

"I'm not ready for you to go, Grandpa," Marcus said. "There was all this stuff we were going to do. Remember that trip to Philadelphia that we kept talking about? You said I couldn't go through life without seeing the Liberty Bell at least once. You said it was the only broken thing worth looking at." He laughed softly. "I'll still see it though. I promise."

He put his head down, and Lena thought he must be crying. But when he finally glanced up again, his face was dry. "You know that book you gave me? I think it helped. So thank you. For that, and for everything. I...I don't know what else to say. Except that I brought you something." He dug in his bag and pulled out the moon ship. "I wanted you to have this. I...I thought it might make you smile."

As he gently placed the model on the table by the bed, Marcus's phone beeped, telling him it was almost time. He let out a long breath and looked at Lena. "I don't know if I can do this," he said.

"You have to, Marcus. Once the soul is assigned to you, you're the only one who can collect it."

Marcus jumped to his feet and went to the window. He struggled to open it, but it wouldn't unlock. "It's not fair. Why would they have me do it? I'm his grandson," Marcus said in a hushed voice, clearly not wanting Grandpa Joe to hear.

"You're right," Lena said, going over to him. "It's not fair. It was probably supposed to be my assignment, but now that you have my powers, they gave it to you."

Suddenly, Marcus's face brightened. "I know, you can zap him! A love boost will give him extra time like it did with Mrs. Katz."

Lena shook her head slowly. "Remember what Eddie said, it's only temporary. And for all we know, the only reason that worked was because the mailman showed up at the right time."

"We'll find a nurse and have the two of them fall in love. If it keeps him alive, then—"

"Marcus," Lena said. "You might give him a few more days, but that's it. I know you don't want to let him go, but it's selfish to keep him here when his soul is ready to move on. It's his time."

Marcus stood there not moving or speaking. She wasn't sure he was still breathing. "I know it doesn't feel like it," Lena added softly, "but you're helping your grandpa. I promise."

He whirled toward her, his face bright red. "How can you even say that? I'm not helping him. I'm *killing* him," Marcus said in a fierce whisper. "Can't you see that? You're like an emotionless robot. No wonder you didn't get into the play."

Lena stared at him in shock. How could he say that to her? She'd thought Marcus really cared about her, but clearly she was wrong.

"You know what?" she said. "Do whatever you want. You're on your own."

She turned to leave the room, but Marcus jumped in front of her. "No, please," he said. "I'm sorry, okay? I don't know why I said that. I didn't mean it." His face crumpled. "Please don't go. I can't...I can't do this by myself."

Lena hesitated. No matter how betrayed she felt, could she really leave Marcus to do this collection on his own? If he chickened out, Grandpa Joe's soul would drift around, totally helpless and confused. She'd never met the man before, but from hearing Marcus talk about him, she knew he was something special. She couldn't let that happen to him.

"Fine," she said. "I'll help you."

His phone started beeping incessantly. Marcus turned it off

and went back to his grandpa's bedside. "Okay," he said softly. "What do I do?"

She went to stand beside him. Her anger at what he'd said was still bubbling in her chest, but she pushed it down. He'd been upset, that was all. Maybe he really hadn't meant it. And besides, she had more important things to think about right now.

"Call up your energy."

He did as she said, and a moment later, his fingers flared purple.

"Now, put your hand on his arm and imagine his soul going off somewhere calm and peaceful. Imagine that you're sending him off on the best vacation ever."

Marcus smiled sadly. "The biggest golf course in the universe. He'd love that."

"Perfect," she said.

She watched as his glowing fingers crept toward Grandpa Joe's hand. Then, slowly, the energy flowed into the old man's skin and disappeared.

Marcus pulled his hand back and slumped, clearly exhausted.

"Are you okay?" Lena asked.

He nodded but didn't say anything.

"It'll happen in the next couple of minutes," she said. "You don't have to be here to see it if you don't want. You did your part."

Marcus shook his head. "No, I want to stay with him… until the end."

He gently took his grandpa's hand again and held it, talking to him in a low murmur that Lena could barely hear. As she watched Marcus saying good-bye, she was surprised to feel tears rolling down her face. She couldn't remember the last time she'd cried, really cried, since her mom had left. That time, she'd been crying for herself. But this time, her tears were for Marcus.

chapter 27

When Grandpa Joe finally slipped away, Marcus was in a daze. He watched as the nurses rushed around, trying to do something, but he knew it was too late. As he and Lena stood in the hallway with his family, for once he was the only one not crying. He didn't need to cry. Because when he'd felt Grandpa's soul leaving, it hadn't been terrible. In fact, he'd felt a sense of relief, as if the soul had finally been set free. And now Grandpa didn't have to be in pain anymore.

Lena had been right. He couldn't keep running from Caspar his whole life, just like he couldn't keep running from everything else he was afraid of. Especially not when Grandpa had needed him to be brave.

"Marcus," Lena said softly. "I think you should be with your family. I'm going to go home, okay?"

"Thank you. For everything. If it wasn't for you, I'd…"

She smiled. "You're welcome. I'll see you tonight, okay?"

He blinked. The party. With everything that had happened, he'd forgotten. But yes, of course he had to go. If this was his chance to swap their powers back, he had to take it. Still, he didn't feel so desperate to get rid of this power anymore, now that he understood what it really was.

"I'll see you tonight," he said.

Once she was gone, his dad came over to him. "Son, are you all right? Did you get to say good-bye?"

Marcus couldn't believe how upset his dad looked, how red his eyes were from crying. Maybe there were times when looking weak didn't matter.

"I'm fine," Marcus said. "Are you guys okay?"

His mom put her arm around Ann-Marie. "We're hanging in there," she said. "Your grandpa always wanted us to be okay, no matter what. You remind me of him, Marcus. You have ever since you were born."

"Really?" Marcus asked.

"Your mother's right," his dad said. "Your grandfather was a good man." Marcus realized, with a shock, that his father had actually paid him a compliment. He couldn't remember the last time that had happened.

His mom let out a soft laugh. "You even look like him when he was your age, Marcus. Did I ever show you photos from when your grandpa was growing up?"

Marcus shook his head.

She sighed. "I'll have to look around in the basement and try to find them."

"Do you have a date with Lena tonight?" Ann-Marie suddenly chimed in. He was ready to be annoyed with her for making fun of him, but she didn't look like she was teasing him. "I like her," she added.

"It's not a date," he said. "Not exactly. But there's this party tonight—"

"Party?" His dad pursed his lips. "You're not going to a party. Not with everything that's happened. How would that look?"

"But you don't understand. I have to go."

"We'll talk about this later," his mom interrupted. "Let's go home, okay?"

Normally, Marcus would have let his mom brush the topic aside. Then he'd give in when his parents forbade him from doing whatever it was he wanted to do. But this time, he wasn't going to let that happen. Not when this was so important.

"No. We're going to talk about it now."

His dad raised his eyebrows. "Marcus—"

"Please, listen," Marcus said. "When I said I have to go to this party, I meant it. I made a promise, okay? I can't break it. You're always going on about being a man and honoring the family and all of that. Doesn't that mean keeping promises?"

His dad looked at him.

"You know how much I love Grandpa," Marcus went on. "I would never go to a party on a day like this if I didn't have to. But it's important. Please trust me."

His dad gave him a long look, and Marcus waited for the explosion to come. But it didn't. Instead, his dad looked at him with an expression Marcus had only seen him give his sister, one of respect.

"All right," his dad said. "But don't stay too long, okay?"

"I won't." If all went according to plan, Marcus would only need five seconds.

chapter 28

Connie Reynolds's house was exactly like it had been the previous weekend. Music echoed up from the basement windows while kids milled around in the front yard, waiting for their friends to arrive. Once again, someone had tied an oversized bouquet of balloons to the Reynoldses' mailbox that threatened to pull the whole thing out of the ground.

Had the last party happened only six days ago? It felt like a lifetime had gone by since Lena had had her old powers.

"There you are," Abigail said when they met in Connie's driveway. "I was starting to think you weren't coming." It was exactly what she'd said to Lena the last time.

"How was play practice today?" Lena asked as they headed toward the basement stairs.

"Oh, it was good." It sounded like Abigail wanted to say more, but she didn't go on.

"What?" Lena asked finally. "Why are you being weird?"

"Nothing. It's only...I figured you didn't really want to hear about the play since it's a sore topic and everything."

It was a sore topic, but after everything that had happened today, it didn't seem as important. Abigail was obviously the best actress in their grade. She deserved to be in the play. "I don't mind if you talk about it," Lena told her. "Honest. Besides, I'm going to work my butt off so that next time, I *will* get in."

Abigail smiled. "Well, if you really want to hear about it... the first day was awesome!" Then she recapped how the read-through had gone and declared that it was going to be the school's most amazing production ever.

As the two of them wove through the basement, Lena was overwhelmed all over again by the loudness of the crowd. A boy from her science class was (yet again) banging away on a drum set in the corner, making the floor shake. Most of the kids were even wearing the same outfits they'd had on the previous weekend.

"I can't believe this is so much like last time," Lena said, shaking her head in wonder.

"Last time?" Abigail asked.

"Yeah, Connie's party last weekend. Remember?"

Abigail blinked. "Oh yeah. Funny that she's having another one so soon." Then she shrugged, the topic clearly forgotten.

Lena smothered a smile. Eddie really had worked some kind of magic. Wait, why was she thinking about magic of all things? But then again, she wasn't sure what else to call it. Science really couldn't explain the fact that everything was almost exactly as it had been a week ago.

"I'm going to go see if Marcus is here," Lena said.

Abigail gave Lena a knowing smile. Then she glanced down at her flashing phone. "It's Hayleigh. She's in the bathroom having some kind of glitter emergency. How about I go help her and you go find Marcus?"

Lena went over to the snack table, scanning the crowd for Brent Adamson. Thankfully, like last time, he wasn't in attendance. She'd feel terrible if he got sick in the middle of a party because of her.

As she realized that she was standing next to the bowl of Cheetos, déjà vu washed over her. What had she been doing at the party last Saturday? That's right. She'd been counting the seconds until Abigail and Hayleigh got back from the bathroom.

She put a Cheeto in her mouth and started—1, 2, 3—when she heard a familiar voice screech, "You! I dare you to kiss Lena Perris for five seconds."

Lena whirled around, and sure enough, Marcus was there, peering back at her with a smile that felt like it was just for her.

"You want him to *what*?" Lena asked, fighting back a smile of her own.

"Do it," Connie said. "Or I'll make you both lick the toilet."

Lena barely heard the chorus of "oohs" that echoed around her. She was already walking toward Marcus. Before she knew it, they were in the closet and Connie was squawking, "Remember, five seconds!" and shoving the door closed behind them.

"So, do you want to?" Marcus asked.

This time, Lena didn't hesitate. "Okay."

They took a step forward and then another. At first they bumped noses. Then they bumped chins. And the third time, for some reason, they bumped ears. But finally, their lips met and—

Wow, Lena thought. The kiss was perfect. It was exactly what she'd always imagined her first kiss with Brent Adamson would be like.

Then Connie threw open the door, and it was over.

"Well, how was it?" she asked.

But Lena and Marcus didn't answer. Instead, they headed up the stairs and out into the yard. The night air was deafeningly quiet around them.

"Ready?" Lena asked.

Marcus nodded. "I think it worked, don't you?"

They put out their hands and called up their energy. Their fingers flared up in unison and—

"Oh," Lena said as Marcus let out a disappointed sigh beside her. Her fingers were still red and his were still purple. If anything, the colors were even more pronounced than they had been before.

"It didn't work," Marcus said. "I don't get it. We did everything right."

"Maybe we're not meant to switch them back," Lena said. "Maybe they're meant to stay this way from now on. I'm sorry."

"Why are you sorry? It's not your fault."

"No, I'm sorry that you have to keep collecting souls. I know how much you hate it."

"It…it wasn't as bad as I thought. You were right. It's how things work. *I'm* sorry you have to make people think they're in love."

She smiled. "Maybe it's not always pretend. Maybe sometimes it's real."

Just then, someone whistled nearby, and a second later, Eddie rolled up on a pair of sleek, silver roller skates. "Well?" he asked. "Any luck?"

They shook their heads, and he let out an annoyed grunt. "Well, shoot," he said. "The boss lady is not going to be happy. Your erratic powers are staring to cause a chain reaction. I

Anna Staniszewski

heard about a couple in France who fell into hate with each other instead of love! And our soul collection numbers are completely off for this time of year."

"Then what do we do?" Marcus asked.

Eddie's shoulders sagged. "I honestly don't know. If this did not work, then…"

"We're stuck like this," Lena said, even though she knew they were all thinking it.

"Does that mean we'll never be able to touch anyone again without worrying about hurting them?" Marcus asked.

"And that every time we mess up, even more people might get hurt?" Lena asked. Seeing Professor playing house with a squirrel was bad enough, not to mention everything that had happened with her dad and with Brent, but if people all over the world were starting to suffer because of her mistakes, that was too much to handle.

"I won't give up, okay?" Eddie said, chewing on his lip. "There has to be something we haven't tried yet."

Lena could tell he was trying to be positive, but it all sounded hopeless.

chapter 29

Marcus couldn't remember the last time his family had all had breakfast together. Normally, his dad and Ann-Marie were at the track before dawn, practicing. And usually their kitchen table was covered in uniforms and protein bars and sports magazines. But this morning, Marcus and his family sat at the kitchen table, eating pancakes and talking about what Grandpa would have wanted for his funeral.

After Marcus had come home last night, he'd finally gotten up the courage to throw away the terrarium in his room. He didn't need it to remind him of his turtle, not when he had years of memories to tap into. When his mom had seen what he'd done, she'd given him a sad smile and said, "Maybe we all need to declutter our lives a little." Then she'd moved some of the junk out of the basement so that his dad could bring a few of the weight machines downstairs. Now the house was neater than it had been in years. Marcus had even spotted one of his own school pictures hanging on a wall that used to be hidden by a treadmill.

He also seemed to have a new pet in his life. All morning, he'd been hearing meowing. And now, as he sat at breakfast, he felt the ghost cat rubbing up against his leg. That was certainly going to take some getting used to.

"I'm going to cut a bunch of roses from my garden for the memorial service," Ann-Marie announced when they were done eating. Marcus expected her to complain that her prized red roses were gone thanks to him, but she only added, "Grandpa always said the pink ones were his favorite."

"That's a lovely idea," his mom said. "Do you want to help her, Marcus?"

"I have to go meet Lena for a little while, but I'll help when I get back."

"You really like this girl, don't you?" his mom asked.

He stared down at his empty plate, sure that his ears were turning red.

"Aw, leave the boy alone," his dad said. "He can have his secrets."

Marcus practically fell out of his chair to hear his dad standing up for him. Maybe after everything that had happened yesterday, he'd gained a little respect for his son. Or, more likely, he was glad that Marcus was finally showing an interest in girls.

When breakfast was over, Marcus went to get ready. He was relieved to see that the bruises on his face had finally faded and that he looked like himself again. As he ran a comb through his hair, he heard meowing coming from outside his bedroom door. He opened the door, and a flicker of light came bounding into his room and hopped up on his bed.

Marcus watched as it curled up on his pillow and then lay motionless. A moment later, he thought he could hear faint purring. A ghost cat wasn't exactly the kind of pet he'd always dreamed of, but the creature had had a tough life when it had been alive. Why not give it a good home while its soul was still here? At least he didn't have to worry about remembering to feed it or his sister being allergic like she was to regular cats.

He grabbed Grandpa Joe's dating book and slipped it into his pocket, desperate to have part of Grandpa with him today. Then he gave himself one more check in the mirror and headed out to the park to meet Lena.

A few minutes later, when Marcus got to the bench where he'd first seen Olivia, a shiver went through him. He still had that dangerous power inside him. If he messed up, someone else might get hurt. But he'd also used it to help others. He would have to remember that when he got too freaked out.

"You're here!" Lena said, and he couldn't help grinning as her face lit up. She was genuinely happy to see him, but when he lingered for a moment, thinking about leaning in for a kiss, she took a visible step backward.

Marcus felt a stab in his chest, but he tried to ignore it. He was starting to think Lena did like him, but maybe she wasn't ready to admit it to herself yet. That was okay for now. He'd already been waiting since last spring. He could wait a little longer.

As they sat down on the bench together, he couldn't help boasting, "I read the whole soul-collecting manual last night. It made everything sound a lot less scary."

"See? I told you."

"How's your dad doing?" Marcus asked.

Lena sighed. "Marguerite's blowing him off again. I tried to convince him that he should go over there to see her today, but I don't think it worked. I know I shouldn't zap them again, but…"

"Sometimes you have to let these things go."

She sighed again. "I know. I guess I was hoping, now that he's finally happy, he could stay that way."

"Maybe she's not the right match for him."

"Maybe." He could tell she didn't like the idea, but he had to remind himself that she was new to this matchmaking thing. Eventually she'd understand that you couldn't force people to fall in love. It was up to them.

"At least my dog is still happy," Lena said. "He and the

squirrel are building a nest right behind our house. My dad is even talking about doing a scientific study on unusual animal behavior."

Marcus laughed. "I guess sometimes you do get a happy ending, even in real life."

Just then, Lena's phone started to ring. She frowned as she saw it was Abigail calling. "She's supposed to be at Saturday play rehearsal." She answered the phone and listened for a long time, her eyes getting rounder and rounder. "Okay, I'll be right there!" she practically shrieked before hanging up the phone.

"What's going on?"

"Two of the playing cards in the show got mono and had to drop out. Mr. Jackson's holding emergency auditions this afternoon to replace them."

"That's great!" Marcus said. "Er, not about the mono. But this is your chance to rock your audition." He smiled. "Isn't mono called the kissing disease?" There was something kind of perfect about that.

But Lena wasn't smiling. "What if I mess up again? What if—"

"You'll be fine. I'll be there the whole time. Okay?"

She nodded. "But we have to hurry. The audition starts in an hour." She jumped to her feet and practically ran out of the park, Marcus hurrying after her.

chapter 30

"Are there more kids coming?" Lena asked Abigail, surprised at how few people were in the auditorium.

Abigail shook her head. "Mr. Jackson only invited a few people back to audition, the ones who were really close to making it in the first time. He wanted to call you, but I begged him to let me do it. I knew you'd freak out!"

Lena looked at Mr. Jackson across the room. He flashed her a reassuring smile, like he believed she deserved to be there. She had to show him that he was right to give her another chance.

Abigail gave Marcus a wave. "Are you auditioning too?"

He laughed. "No way. The last time I auditioned for anything, I peed my pants." His cheeks went pink. "I was, um, in kindergarten."

Lena cringed and explained, "He's here for moral support." No doubt Abigail would go back to making fun of Marcus behind his back after this.

She was surprised though, when Abigail laughed and said to Marcus, "Don't tell anyone, but the first time I had to talk in front of the whole class in first grade, I was so nervous that I cried in the bathroom beforehand."

Marcus smiled his bright, infectious smile. "Well, it looks like you've gotten a little better at the whole public speaking thing. I heard you're awesome in the play."

Abigail shrugged at the compliment, but Lena could tell she was flattered.

"If you need to go cry in the bathroom on opening night though, we'll cover for you," Marcus added.

Abigail laughed and flashed Lena a look that she could only describe as "approving." Finally, her friend was getting a glimpse of the nonweirdo Marcus that Lena had gotten to know.

Just then, she spotted Brent Adamson on the other side of the auditorium, lugging in some sets for the play. Oh no. Before she could duck out of the way, Brent's eyes met hers. Lena waited for him to drop his end of the set and go running off to the bathroom. Instead, he stopped and cringed. His face looked a little pale, but it wasn't green. Then he shook his head and went back to pulling the set piece.

"Did you see that?" Lena whispered to Marcus.

He nodded. "I think it's finally fading."

"Thank goodness!" Lena said. "I was starting to think I'd have to wear a mask all the time or something."

"All right, folks," Mr. Jackson called. "Let's begin! Those of you auditioning, go wait in the wings."

"Break a leg," Abigail whispered as she walked by.

Even though Marcus wasn't technically allowed to, Lena had him follow her up onto the stage. She read over the monologue, the same one she'd used for the first audition. The one she'd royally messed up. Suddenly, her whole body started shaking, like there was a tiny earthquake going on inside of her. What if she messed up even worse this time? That would prove that she didn't have what it took to be a real actress one day.

When they found a spot in the dimly lit wings, she turned to Marcus and said in a panicked whisper, "What if you're right and I am some kind of robot? Maybe that's why I didn't get in the first time. You and Mr. Jackson both said I was stiff. Maybe I can't act at all!"

Marcus shook his head. "You can do this. Ever since all this stuff happened to us, you've been so different. So much more *you*. Just be that way onstage."

Lena closed her eyes. He was right. Ever since their powers had swapped, she'd been struggling to push down all the emotions swirling inside of her. But she'd been failing, as if all those feelings were leaking out of her no matter how much she tried to hold them in. She'd even cried at the hospital yesterday! Lena couldn't remember the last time she'd lost control like that. Maybe that's what Marcus meant when he said she'd become more like herself.

She'd told him that he needed to stop running, but the truth was, she'd been running too. From her feelings. From the possibility of getting hurt or losing control. But actresses had to embrace all of those things or they'd never be any good.

"Thanks," she said. And then she did something she would have never expected. She leaned forward and kissed Marcus right there in the wings, in front of everyone.

The minute their lips touched, energy zinged through her from the top of her skull all the way to the bottoms of her heels.

"Wow," they both whispered. Then Lena's eyes popped open, and she gasped as she realized that the air around them was *glowing*.

"Did you feel that?" Marcus asked.

Lena nodded. She glanced down and thought she even saw a wisp of smoke coming out of her shoes. Could this mean…? Was it possible…?

"Lena Perris!" Mr. Jackson. "You're next!"

She staggered back, her entire body thrumming with electricity.

"Lena? Are you there?"

"I'm-I'm coming!" she called, stumbling onto the stage. She could barely think, barely breathe. She felt electric. She tried to calm herself down, tried to push the giddiness away so she could focus on her audition piece. But then it hit her. Why should she push it away? Why shouldn't she use it? After all, it was what she was feeling.

As she stood in the middle of the stage, she didn't only say the words. She became Alice. Scared, excited, overwhelmed Alice. She let herself feel every line, every word, until it seemed like they were part of her.

And then, finally, it was over.

"Great job, Lena!" Mr. Jackson called from the front row while the other kids clapped. "Tremendous improvement!"

Lena felt her face glowing with excitement. When she went into the wings, she saw Marcus waiting for her with that same glow on his face.

"You were amazing," he whispered.

"It worked, didn't it?" she said. "We're back to normal!"

He smiled. "I think so."

Together, they snuck out the side stage door and into the hallway. Then, when they were sure no one was looking, they called up their energy.

Marcus's was a bright red. Lena's was a deep purple. Exactly like they were supposed to be.

"It worked!" Lena threw her arms around Marcus and squeezed him until her muscles ached.

"But how?" Marcus asked. "What did we do differently?"

"I don't know." Lena's whole body was still dancing with energy. "It had to be something that we missed at the party."

"We did everything the same way."

Lena frowned. "Maybe that was the problem. We let Connie push us into that closet, just like the first time. And we let Eddie do it too."

"What do you mean?"

"Aren't you always saying that you can't force love? Well, maybe we couldn't force our powers to swap back. We had to kiss because we wanted to, not because someone was making us."

And then it hit her. She'd kissed Marcus because she'd wanted to. She hadn't been scared of feeling something for him, of being a weak, mushy girl. Because being with Marcus didn't make her feel that way. It made her feel more like herself. She'd been jealous of her dad having Marguerite to laugh with and talk to, but the truth was, Lena already had those things with Marcus. She'd just been too scared to admit it to herself until now.

"I can't believe it's really over," Marcus said. "Do you feel all back to normal?"

"No, I feel better. Like I could do anything."

They heard Mr. Jackson through the auditorium door asking everyone to gather around.

"Sounds like he's going to announce his decision," Marcus said.

"Wish me luck," she said. Then she grabbed his hand and pulled him into the auditorium.

"Ah, Lena, there you are," Mr. Jackson said. "I was about to announce that you, young lady, are one of our new playing cards!"

Lena whooped with joy. This was the moment she'd been dreaming of for years. Being onstage. Being an actress. It was finally happening. And it was only the beginning.

chapter 31

Lena was still beaming on her way home. Her happiness dimmed though, when she thought about what her returning powers might mean for Mrs. Katz. Was the old woman's extra time finally up?

She pulled to a stop across the street from the old woman's house and was surprised to find Mrs. Katz and the mailman outside in the garden, happily pulling weeds. As she watched them laughing together, the air around Mrs. Katz shifted, and Lena caught a glimpse of her soul. It was faint and wispy, barely clinging to the old woman's body. It wouldn't hold on for much longer. Mrs. Katz probably had a day, maybe two, left.

Should she warn Mrs. Katz how short her time was? As Lena watched the woman tuck a flower behind the mailman's ear, she decided not to. Even if Mrs. Katz only had a couple of days left, they would be happy ones that she never would have had if this whole power-swapping mess hadn't happened. Let her enjoy the time she had left without worrying about what came next.

Lena gave Mrs. Katz one last look, knowing she'd probably be visiting her again soon, and headed for home.

She found her dad slumped on the couch, watching some boring show about rocks. She didn't need Marcus's powers to tell her that the gray cloud of loneliness was back.

"Dad, are you okay?"

"Sure, Lena. I'm great." She couldn't help noticing that he'd stopped calling her Chipmunk again.

"Dad," she said, sitting down next to him. "I'm worried about you."

"About me? Why?"

"Because you keep pretending you're fine, but you're not. I thought having Marguerite around would help, but now you're miserable again."

"Lena, you don't need to worry about me. I'll figure things out."

"But I can't help worrying. And if you pretend you're fine when you're not, then what's to keep me from doing it? Then we'll just be lying to each other." She sighed. "In fact, I think we've already been doing that. Ever since Mom left, we've barely talked about it. And we've both been taking all our sadness and putting it into these little boxes, hoping it'll go away. We can't do that anymore. I *won't*."

Her dad looked at her for a long while. "I thought you were doing all right."

"So did I," she said. "But that's why I couldn't get into the play, because I forgot what it was like to actually feel things. I was pretending, and so are you."

"I've wanted to be strong for you. I thought if I was all right, then you would be too."

"Can't we both be honest?" she asked.

He nodded and took a sip of coffee. Real coffee, Lena realized. Not just hot water.

"All right," her dad said. Then he laughed suddenly. "You know, I realized that I must have been pretty lonely to go to all that trouble to get Marguerite to go out with me again. I wouldn't have pursued her otherwise."

"Really? But you guys have so much in common. It seemed like the perfect match."

"I thought so too at first. The only trouble is that I hate scientists. They're boring." He laughed again. "I know how that sounds. But can you imagine me talking to someone exactly like me for hours? We'd bore each other to tears. I need someone who's interested in other things. That's why your mom and I worked so well together, at least for a while."

"So you'll try dating again?" she asked. "Even though it's all just brain chemicals?"

"The science is part of it, of course. But maybe I've been oversimplifying a bit because it made me feel better after what happened with your mom. Love might be chemicals, but it's more than that. And honestly, I think I've done enough moping around. It's time for me to have a life again." He chuckled as Professor let out a joyful bark in the backyard. "If our old dog can find love, then I think any of us can."

"As long as you don't have a date the first weekend of December," Lena said. "Because you're coming to see me in the school play."

Her dad's face lit up. "What? You got in after all?"

She told him about the emergency auditions—without mentioning the supernatural stuff, of course. "I'm going to be a playing card! I only have one line, but it's a whole line! You'll get to hear me speak onstage!" She was giddy just thinking about it.

"Wow, Chipmunk. I can't remember the last time I saw you this excited."

Lena laughed. She couldn't remember the last time she'd *felt* this excited.

Her phone beeped, and Lena grinned wider when she saw it was a message from Marcus.

"Who's that?" her dad asked.

"My boyfriend," Lena said. Then she froze in shock as she realized the words that had come out of her mouth. She had a boyfriend. A real one! Wait until she marked that in her calendar! Okay, it didn't seem fair that "get into the school play" and "first boyfriend" would fall on the same day. Or maybe it was more than fair. After all, how lucky could one person get? At this rate, she'd be done with her checklist in no time. Even though she had to admit that it didn't seem all that important anymore.

"Boyfriend, huh?" her dad said. "And what does this boyfriend of yours have to say?"

She opened the message, and her stomach sank as she read it.

Meet me at the hospital. It's Olivia.

Lena prepared herself for the worst. Who knew what their powers swapping back might have done to Olivia?

But when she got out of the hospital elevator, she was surprised to hear what sounded like a party coming from Olivia's room, people laughing and chatting. She poked her head in and spotted Marcus sitting on a chair, talking with a redheaded man who looked vaguely familiar. But most important, Olivia was sitting up in her bed and laughing along with them. She was awake!

"There you are," Marcus said, catching sight of her. "Keith, Olivia, this is Lena. She's the one I was telling you about. My, um—"

"His girlfriend," Lena said, which made Marcus beam back at her so brightly he could have been a supernova.

"It's so nice to meet you," Olivia said. "Marcus has been singing your praises. Thank you for helping me in the park that day."

Lena shot Marcus a questioning look. What was going on here?

"Olivia woke up yesterday," Marcus explained. "And the doctors say if everything stays the same, she'll be able to go home next week."

"Wow, really?" Lena said. "That's great."

"Then maybe the two of us can have our first official date," Keith said, taking Olivia's hand.

Suddenly, Lena recognized him. He was the redheaded man who'd called 911 that day in the park.

Marcus smiled and gave Lena a knowing nod. She couldn't believe it. Even though these two hadn't been zapped with a "love boost," they'd somehow wound up falling in love with each other? Lena remembered the spark she thought she'd seen in Olivia's chest. It hadn't been her imagination after all.

"But how?" she asked. "You were in a coma!"

Olivia laughed. "I'm not sure. Keith said he sat here and read to me for hours. And when I woke up, I felt like I'd known him for years, even though I'd never seen him before."

"I can't explain it, but I just knew I had to be here when she woke up." Keith shrugged. "It's one of life's mysteries, I guess."

"Maybe it was supposed to work out this way," Marcus said.

Lena shook her head in wonder. Maybe it all was.

epilogue

E ddie stood outside the hospital room, listening to Lena and Marcus chatting with the young woman and her new match. He was relieved it had finally all worked out. If the mess had dragged on for a day longer, no doubt he would have been on probation again, not to mention all the irreparable damage it could have caused. He had his hands full as it was, putting everything back in order.

He grabbed his phone and dialed. "Yes, ma'am," he said when someone answered. "Both love matches were successful, after everything."

He paced around the hallway, listening. He wasn't sure how Marcus and Lena had managed a love match for Olivia when neither of them had even zapped her, but he wasn't going to question it. One thing he'd learned on the job over the years was that you could always count on surprises. For example, the love match between Lena and Marcus suddenly working out after all this time had been a shock. They'd been zapped last spring during their math project, and nothing had come of it. Eddie had figured it wasn't meant to work out. But maybe they simply needed to spend more time with one another. Or maybe they needed all this craziness to bring them together. Whatever it was, he was happy for them. He only hoped they were strong enough to handle what was coming next.

The voice on the other end of the phone grew louder, and Eddie realized he hadn't been paying attention. "What was that, ma'am?" He listened again for a long while, and then he sighed. "Well, they think everything is back to normal. I thought I would let them enjoy things for a little while before I turn their worlds upside down again." He sighed again. "They will have plenty to deal with soon enough."

acknowledgments

My thanks to L. M. Boston for her haunting novel *The Children of Green Knowe*; its mention of a play in which Cupid and Death accidentally swap arrows inspired the premise of this book. Thank you to Heather Kelly, Megan Kudrolli, Susan Lubner, Susan L. Meyer, Patty Bovie, and Josh Funk for their feedback and brainstorming help. As always, thank you to Ammi-Joan Paquette and Aubrey Poole for constantly pushing me to make my work better, and to my family and friends for continuing to wave their pom-poms book after book. And thank you to Ray Brierly, to whom this book is dedicated, for reading more versions of my novels than anyone should ever be forced to and for slipping me pieces of chocolate when I need them the most.

about the author

Anna Staniszewski lives outside Boston with her wacky dog and her slightly less wacky husband. She was a Writer-in-Residence at the Boston Public Library and a winner of the PEN New England Discovery Award. When she's not writing, Anna teaches, reads, and tries to keep her magical powers under wraps. Visit her at www.annastan.com.

Watch out for the next book in the
Switched at First Kiss series:

FINDERS REAPERS

Anna Staniszewski

THE FUTURE OF LOVE AND DEATH DEPENDS ON A BUDDING TWEEN ROMANCE...WHAT COULD POSSIBLY GO WRONG?

After their power-swapping ordeal, cupid Marcus and reaper Lena can't wait for things to return to (relative) normal. There's just one problem: their powers are now intertwined, and the fate of all future matches and soul collections depend on them getting along in their budding new romance.

But when Lena catches Adelaid, the brand-new soul collector in town, flirting with Marcus, emotions start to go haywire and so do their assignments. Marcus and Lena know they need to work together, but there's more at stake than either supernatural tween imagined...

THE DIRT DIARY SERIES

Anna Staniszewski

The Dirt Diary

EIGHTH GRADE NEVER SMELLED SO BAD.

Rachel Lee didn't think anything could be worse than her parents splitting up. She was wrong. Working for her mom's new house-cleaning business puts Rachel in the dirty bathrooms of the most popular kids in the eighth grade. Which does not help her already loserish reputation. But her new job has surprising perks: enough dirt on the in-crowd to fill up her (until recently) boring diary. She never intended to reveal her secrets, but when the hottest guy in school pays her to spy on his girlfriend, Rachel decides to get her hands dirty.

The Prank List

Anna Staniszewski

TO SAVE HER MOM'S CLEANING BUSINESS, RACHEL'S ABOUT TO GET HER HANDS DIRTY—AGAIN.

Rachel Lee is having the best summer ever taking a baking class and flirting with her almost-sort-of-boyfriend Evan—until a rival cleaning business swoops into town, stealing her mom's clients. Rachel never thought she'd fight for the right to clean toilets, but she has to save her mom's business. Nothing can distract her from her mission...except maybe Whit, the cute new guy in cooking class. Then she discovers something about Whit that could change everything. After destroying her Dirt Diary, Rachel thought she was done with secrets, but to save her family's business, Rachel's going to have to get her hands dirty. Again.

The Gossip File

Anna Staniszewski

SOME THINGS ARE BEST KEPT SECRET...

Rachel is spending the holiday break with her dad and soon-to-be step-monster, Ellie. Thank goodness her BFF Marisol gets to come with. But when Rachel meets a new group of kids and realizes she can leave her loser status back home, quirky Marisol gets left behind. Bored and abandoned, Marisol starts a Gossip File, collecting info on the locals. When the gossip includes some dirt on Ellie, Rachel has to decide if getting the truth is worth risking her new cool-girl persona...

THE
MY VERY UNFAIRY
TALE LIFE SERIES
Anna Staniszewski

My Very UnFairy Tale Life

THIS IS ONE DAMSEL THAT DOESN'T NEED RESCUING.

Jenny has spent the last two years as an adventurer helping magical kingdoms around the universe. But it's a thankless job, leaving her no time for school or friends. She'd almost rather take a math test than rescue yet another magical creature! When Jenny is sent on yet another mission, she has a tough choice to make: quit and have her normal life back, or fulfill her promise and go into a battle she doesn't think she can win.

My Epic Fairy Tale Fail

FAIRY TALES DO COME TRUE. UNFORTUNATELY.

Jenny has finally accepted her life of magic and mayhem as savior of fairy tale kingdoms, but that doesn't mean the job's any easier. Her new mission is to travel to the Land of Tales to defeat an evil witch and complete three Impossible Tasks. Throw in some school friends, a bumbling knight, a rhyming troll, and a giant bird, and happily ever after starts looking far, far away. But with her parents' fate on the line, this is one happy ending Jenny is determined to deliver.

My Sort of Fairy Tale Ending

HAPPILY EVER AFTER? YEAH, RIGHT.

Jenny's search for her parents leads her to Fairyland, a rundown amusement park filled with creepily happy fairies and disgruntled leprechauns. Despite the fairies' kindness, she knows they are keeping her parents from her. If only they would stop being so happy all the time—it's starting to weird her out! With the help of a fairy-boy and some rebellious leprechauns, Jenny finds a way to rescue her parents, but at the expense of putting all magical worlds in danger. Now Jenny must decide how far she is willing to go to put her family back together.